I0766952

His Coffee Shop Crush

A Rosedale Novel

Elle Waters

This is a work of fiction. Names, places, organizations, and events are either products of the author's imagination or are used entirely fictitiously.

Copyright © 2023 by Elle Waters

All rights reserved.

No part of this book may be reproduced in any form or by any electronic or mechanical means, including information storage and retrieval systems, without written permission from the author, except for the use of brief quotations in a book review.

Also by Elle Waters

His Birthday Wish

His Christmas Love Song

His Fake Wedding Date

New Beginnings

Day Dreaming

His Ever After Collection

Rosedale Novels

His Coffee Shop Crush

Cool for the Summer

Autumn Crush

Winter Under the Covers

A Small Town Spring

For Bea

Chapter 1

Jack had been in Rosedale for all of an hour when he decided he'd made a terrible mistake. He never should have listened to Kingston, his agent, when he'd offered his country place for Jack to use until he finished the draft of his book.

He should have stayed in his apartment in New York, with the city noise outside his apartment window constantly present even with noise-canceling headphones, yanking each word out of his soul with a pair of tweezers.

Who cared if his apartment didn't have air conditioning and the city had been having a mid-July heat wave? Who cared if he hadn't been able to finish the manuscript that was due August first? New York was familiar, New York was home, or had been since he moved there from Texas for college over a decade ago.

Rosedale, Connecticut, was only two hours away from Manhattan but it could have been two continents away for all Jack found the endless green trees that surrounded Kingston's cottage unfamiliar and unsettling. Not a single car had passed on the little two-lane road since Jack had arrived in his rented sedan. The silence was unbearable. He wanted to text Kingston that he was heading back to the city, but his agent's words from their conversation a few days ago were still ringing in his head.

"You can't miss another deadline, or they'll cancel your contract and no one is going to pick you up. You can't disappoint your readers like that. They're all looking forward to the next Super Rupert book. And you are going to finish your draft by August first if it kills you—or I'll kill you myself."

Kingston was many things—a great agent, a bit of a foodie, and way too into paisley—but he did not make idle threats. Jack knew he was right—not only did he owe it to the publisher, to his agent, and to himself, but more than anything he owed it to the kids who'd made the Super Rupert middle grade series a hit. He owed them the next book about the adventures of the thirteen-year-old who thought he had superpowers but only had a really good imagination. He was also gay and had a crush on the most popular boy in his school. The fact that Rupert was gay was incidental to the plot of each story, but the way Jack wrote about Rupert's crush, as if it was no different from any thirteen-year-old's crush, had been hailed for its authenticity. The book series had been both lauded for its handling of middle schooler issues and decried by hate groups for sneaking a "gay agenda" into an otherwise universal story.

Jack did think Super Rupert was universal. And even though he'd been creatively blocked as he attempted to write the fourth book in the series, he still believed the books were important. He needed to write.

Kingston had sent him up here to focus and write without distraction. The problem was, Jack needed a little noise to get his creative juices flowing. He looked at his phone. Sighed. He'd never hear the end of it from Kingston if he gave up after one measly hour in the country. Instead, he opened the maps app on his phone and searched "coffee shop."

He found the usual smattering of chain places on the road from Rosedale to the next medium-sized city. One place caught his eye, in the cute downtown area—yes, he could admit to finding the narrow strip of downtown Rosedale cute. Hot Brew. Open until 8. Perfect.

He grabbed his laptop bag and drove the seven minutes to town. He parked on a side street, then found Hot Brew—a narrow storefront on the main drag between a barbecue takeout joint and a secondhand clothes store.

Two young women were leaving the place as he walked in and took stock. There were a few cafe tables near the window and a few more lined the wall beside the coffee bar and register.

Promising.

Two were filled with patrons chatting and he spotted one right next to an outlet. The air smelled strongly of coffee and there were a decent number of baked goods for sale, even this late in the day. The music was audible, but not deafening. He took a minute to place the voice on the sound system. Nina Simone. Even more promising.

He walked up to the counter. A young woman with an eyebrow piercing and pancake makeup that made her pale skin even lighter greeted him with a smile.

"What can I get you?"

He scanned the white lettering on the black chalk board behind her. He usually didn't drink coffee this late in the day, but this seemed like an emergency. If he didn't get at least a few pages written today, that deadline was going to seem even less attainable. "Americano," he decided. "And a bear claw. For here."

Since his thirty second birthday he'd noticed the pastries he loved so much didn't simply melt off him the way they used to. But again. Emergency.

"Name for the order?"

"Jack."

He watched the woman as she rang him up, her black shirt and pants could either have been personal style, or a uniform, but the black apron was definitely mandated, because he saw another employee working the espresso machine who was wearing the same thing. Where the girl was small and pale, this guy, his back to Jack, was tall, slim, with skin tanned the same buttery brown as the top of the croissants in the pastry case. His dark hair brushed the collar of his black T- shirt, and his mile-long legs were encased in skinny black jeans. Okay, maybe black was a theme of this place.

Jack waited by the counter instead of setting up his computer, unwilling to give up an extra minute of procrastination. The woman who waited on him deposited the bear claw on a plate at his elbow, and then the guy at the espresso machine turned around, bearing a white mug.

"Jack?"

The guy's face was a collection of angles that shouldn't have complimented each other, pointed chin, high cheekbones, squinty eyes, and a short nose. Somehow it all combined to make an appealing, intriguing face. His mouth was pretty, and forming Jack's name, it was even prettier. His voice was a low drawl that reminded Jack of home. Not New York, but farther back. Sun-baked sidewalks and freshly mown grass and the murmur of good-old-boys sipping beer while sitting on their trucks' open tailgates.

But this was no good-old-boy. He was a golden-skinned god with mischievous eyes and hair that begged to be played with and pulled. Probably straight. Story of Jack's life.

The guy's smile faded as he repeated the name uncertainly. "Jack?"

Jack blinked. "Sorry, lost in thought." He reached for the cup, realized he couldn't manage it and the bear claw and his heavy computer bag all at once. The guy seemed to notice his predicament, pulled the Americano out of Jack's reach and walked around the counter.

Pull yourself together, he told himself. He saw hot guys six times a day in the city. There was no reason to get all twitterpated over the first guy he saw in small-town Connecticut. Still, as he claimed a table near an outlet and a window, the guy helpfully bringing him a napkin along with his drink, he had to wonder if he was just looking for a distraction, or if the attraction was real. Maybe a bit of both. He hadn't been this immediately attracted to anyone in a long time. He'd almost forgotten the rush of adrenaline, nerves, and excitement, a tantalizing cocktail that made him more useless than usual at regular-person conversation.

"Thanks," he finally muttered once the guy stepped back. "My head's somewhere else today."

"It's fine. The Americano should fix you right up." There was definitely a southern twang in the voice. Jack wondered what he was doing in Yankee country.

He managed a smile. He didn't know why the golden man was still talking to him, but he'd take the extra distraction. "I'm counting on it."

"Cool. I'm Pete. Let me know if you need a refill."

Pete. It had been too long since Jack had been laid if he even thought this guy's name was sexy.

"You from Texas, Pete?" he asked, letting some of the twang he'd erased years ago seep back in. The man didn't try to deny it.

"San Antonio," Pete said. "You?"

"Austin." He'd actually grown up in a suburb, but close enough. Pete didn't say anything back, just studied him for a second and Jack had to stop himself from looking down and making sure he was presentable. When he was in work mode, he rarely paid attention to things like what he was wearing. For the drive from the city he'd thrown on shorts and sneakers and a T-shirt that had once been the color of sage but had faded to a muddy gray. Could be worse. Could be better.

"You're far from home," Pete said. "Tourist?"

"Nah. Manhattan's home now. Harlem. Just visiting Rosedale for a few weeks."

Pete's polite-conversation-smile grew bigger, into something positively gleeful. If Jack didn't think he was in trouble before, now he knew it for sure. Pete's smile was little-kid bright, but his dimples and the way his tanned skin stretched over the bones of his gorgeous face made him look all grown up and sexy as hell.

There was no way this guy was single, even if he was interested. But why else would he still be talking to Jack after delivering his rapidly-cooling coffee?

"What?" Jack said, as Pete continued to smile as if he knew something Jack didn't.

"Just that you sound like me—and not just the accent. I came here six months ago after six years in Manhattan. I thought it would be a short visit, but I'm still here."

"Really?" Jack looked out the window onto the main street beyond. The coffee shop was great, but this town was nothing special, from what he could tell. The usual assortment of shops and restaurants. It was less crowded than the city—he hadn't had any trouble finding a parking spot for his rental car. But he didn't see what was so captivating about it that would get him to give up city life.

"I guess I needed a change," Pete said. "But Rosedale's cool. It's got a lot going on. The Rosedale Art Center puts on tons of events and classes. Concerts in the park all summer long. And there's an annual winter festival. Anyway." Pete stopped talking suddenly, as if he realized he sounded like a spokesman from the tourism board.

Jack smiled at him. "Not sure I'll be here long enough to take advantage, but thanks. I'm supposed to be working, anyway."

"What sort of work?" Pete asked, but Jack was saved from having to answer when a group of teenagers came through the doors of Hot Brew, making a beeline for the counter. Pete's coworker gave him an imploring look and Pete threw Jack an apologetic smile. "Gotta go."

Jack just nodded. He'd enjoyed his conversation with the beautiful barista, but even he had to admit he was reaching peak procrastination levels. He took a fortifying sip of the Americano, which was still hot enough, and delicious, followed by two bites of the best bear claw he'd had in a while. Okay, so he'd found his happy place while he was in Rosedale, but he still had to get to work. He opened his laptop, used every ounce of his willpower to navigate to his draft document instead of his email and looked at where he'd left Rupert hanging.

He had the bones of the first half down, but he'd been stuck trying to figure out where to take the arc with his main character, Rupert, and Rupert's crush, Drew, who had been a sometime enemy, sometime ally in the past books in the series.

He was cutting it damn close. He'd already blown through one deadline. The publisher had reached out to the illustrator, who'd agreed to shorten his own window for getting the artwork done, and he'd been given another six weeks. These books weren't terribly long—about thirty thousand words—so he should be able to get the story done in time.

He stared at his screen, but without the same level of dread he'd had the last dozen times he'd tried to write. He felt the caffeine and sugar surge through his blood, and he glanced up to see Pete at the espresso machine, happily working away on the delicate instruments with what Jack now noticed were oversized hands with elegant fingers. He swallowed, his stomach responding with a not-unpleasant flip to both the stimulants and to Pete.

He'd lost sight of Rupert's goal in the story, and Rupert had lost sight of Drew. He needed to make both central again and the emotional core of the story, the thing the readers most responded to, would be restored. He smiled a little as he started typing, the words coming faster than they had in weeks. When he looked up again, his mug and plate were empty, and he'd written two chapters and gone back and rewritten a few key scenes in the first half of the book.

His shoulders were stiff and he needed to pee, but he felt amazing. For the first time he thought he was going to be able to finish the book. And it might even be good.

Outside Hot Brew's window the sky wasn't exactly dark—the summer days were still long—but the streetlights were lit and the traffic on the sidewalk had shifted from the shops to the restaurants. A little Italian place across the street had a small crowd waiting outside.

He glanced at the counter, but Pete was nowhere to be seen. Maybe he'd gone off shift and Jack hadn't noticed. He stood, closed his laptop and stuck it back in his bag. He took his dishes to the counter, caught the eye of Pete's coworker who was wiping down counters.

"Hey, can I leave these?" he asked.

"Sure. Thanks. How was it?" she asked.

"Great. What time do you open?" He wanted to ask what time Pete would next be working, but he knew she wouldn't tell him.

"Seven."

"Cool. I'll be back. I'm Jack by the way," he said, figuring he should ingratiate himself with more than just Pete if he was going to take up residence in the shop.

"Hi Jack. I'm Meadow. And you already met Pete." She said the last bit with an amused smile, which Jack thought boded very well, though if he abided by the golden rule of don't shit where you eat, he should leave Pete alone so he could keep using the coffee shop as his office.

"Nice to meet you, Meadow. And yeah, I met Pete." He let an answering smile grow on his face. Nothing wrong with keeping his options open.

"He's just taking out the trash," Meadow said.

"Okay," Jack said. "Bathroom?"

Meadow jerked her head to the side. "Down the hall at the end."

He spent a minute smoothing down his hair, which was kind of a hopeless task. He had perpetual bedhead unless he used a lot of product.

When he came out of the bathroom, Pete

was back, talking in low tones with Meadow. The rest of the store was empty. He thought he heard Pete say with fond exasperation, "Mind your business," but they stopped talking when Jack appeared in the main room.

"Hey, taking off?" Pete said.

"Yeah." Jack blinked. Pete had removed his apron and was leaning against the counter, a mile-long feast of legs and arms and skin and hair. It was all so tempting Jack knew if he ever had the chance, he wouldn't know where to start. He cleared his throat. He needed to get it together—he needed this coffee shop. "But I'll be back. Got more work done than I thought."

"Must be the view," Meadow said, and Pete cut her a sharp look.

"Or the coffee," Pete suggested.

"Yeah, the coffee was great. Thanks. Well." Jack shifted his bag. He didn't exactly have anywhere to be, but he couldn't stay here all night pseudo-flirting with Pete while Meadow refereed. "See you later."

"See ya, Jack," Pete said. And that was that.

Jack walked out of Hot Brew, the humidity of the summer's day backing off now that the sun had gone down. He realized he was hungry. A bear claw wasn't dinner, and he had some vague ideas of grocery shopping earlier but had forgotten. Tomorrow, he decided, when he paused in front of the Italian place. A mouthwatering smell came from inside, and suddenly the only thing he could think of was garlicky pasta and tomatoes. He glanced back at the coffee shop, wondering if Pete had dinner plans, but he could only see Meadow inside, wiping down tables.

He suddenly had a wave of homesickness, which was extraordinary. He was thirty-two. He didn't get homesick. And he couldn't put his finger on what exactly he was homesick for. Not New York —he'd be back there soon enough. He glanced back and forth from Hot Brew to the restaurant—Nina's, the sign said. He finally shook himself out of it. He couldn't be homesick for a person that he'd just met—

that was ridiculous. He was maybe a little lonely, that's all. Kingston had promised to come up and visit him if he was making progress on the book. Otherwise, Jack had been keeping his head down and not socializing. That's all it was.

The fierce longing to spend more time with the cute barista was nothing more than his overwrought emotions at getting something done on the book. He only felt a tiny bit sorry for himself when he went inside and asked for a table for one.

Chapter 2

Pete wasn't sure what to do with himself after clocking out of his shift. Normally if he didn't have plans to teach at the Art Center, he'd go back to the room he rented from Carol, a math teacher at Rosedale's middle school, and get to work on his computer. The room was fine—a bed, a desk, his own bathroom, and he could comfortably afford it on what he made at the coffee shop—but on a good day it still felt like what it was—a temporary space in someone else's home.

He found the room and the job at Hot Brew

the same day he'd decided that Rosedale was as good a place as any to take a break from the city. As a starving artist he'd had plenty of experience making coffee, and he didn't mind the work, either. There was always something to do, always someone interesting coming through the doors.

Like Jack.

He hesitated at the corner of Main and Spring. Was his most intriguing customer of the day the reason he felt at loose ends? The idea of going back to his room suddenly made him feel claustrophobic. He felt itchy, like he needed to burn off some energy. He'd already worked out that morning, free weights and the treadmill at the community center where he could exercise for free with the retirement crowd. He bent his neck from side to side, rolled his shoulders. Why was he so antsy?

It couldn't be that a disheveled Texas boy had gotten under his skin, could it? He hadn't felt so much as a ping of lust for anyone in months. It was as if he'd left his libido behind in New York.

His restlessness wasn't entirely due to Jack. It was that he wanted to work, and not serving coffee. Despite his impressive resume as a barista, a server, and once, as a model for a friend's life drawing class during a particularly lean period, he'd actually been selling his art for a while, making enough money to keep him in pencils and paper and his snazzy drawing tablet and software while building his portfolio. He even had a semi-steady gig illustrating a series of books.

He was waiting on the next one in the series, but the author was late, which was kind of annoying, not just because he wanted the paycheck, but because he'd turned down a teaching spot at the Art Center's summer program thinking he'd be working on art for the book and now he was twiddling his thumbs.

Maybe that's what he should do with the extra energy—bug Jonathan.

He took the long way back to Carol's and

wondered if he was just kidding himself about Rosedale. Six months ago, desperate to get out of the city and needing a place to lick his wounds, his friend had offered him his weekend house as a temporary refuge. Two weeks later, Pete decided Rosedale was a good place to start over. He'd grown to love the place, but he couldn't lie to himself—he was hiding here.

Jack, who reeked of the city, reminded him that he'd liked his life there, once upon a time. Before Kurt.

He shook his head, rolled his shoulders again. He'd go home and do some pull ups on the bar he'd installed in a doorway and email Jonathan.

He wouldn't think about green-eyed customers who made him feel too big for his skin.

To jonathanavery@super-rupert.com

From k.james@jamesliteraryagency.com

Jack,

I hope you're enjoying the cottage and even more I hope you're working. Looks like I'll have a free weekend coming up, so I'll see you soon. Don't forget to put the trash out Tuesday night.

Kingston

To jackrossavery@yahoo.com
From mamaavery@gmail.com

Hey sweetie, wanted to let you know we're going to book that Caribbean cruise for Christmas. Last chance if you want us to save you a spot. We can even get you a double if you have anyone special you

want to bring with??? Let me know by
Friday.

Love,
Your Mama

To jonathanavery@super-rupert.com
From pj@pjblue-art.com

Hey! Just checking in. I know you're
working and I don't want to bug you.
Okay, maybe I want to bug you a little.
Just wondering if there was anything I
should know about the upcoming story.
Can I get started on anything?

How's your succulent doing, by the way?
I hope you aren't watering it too much.

P.J.

Checking email before he got out of bed was never a good idea. Jack rubbed his eyes and dropped his phone over the side of the bed. It made a dull thud when it hit the rug. He got out of the surprisingly comfortable guest bed, went to the bathroom down the hall, and looked at his reflection in the mirror. That was weird. He was smiling.

Since he wasn't exactly thrilled about Kingston checking in on him or his mama's latest plan to get out of hosting the entire Avery clan for Christmas by taking a cruise, it was probably the email from P.J. that had put a smile on his face. Which was strange because he didn't even know the guy.

When he'd gotten the contract for the first Super Rupert book, he'd been a newbie to publishing. He hadn't realized until Kingston explained it to him that most publishers had their own relationships with illustrators and artists and the powers that be would choose the artist. An author, especially a first-time, unproven author, didn't have any say at all. Kingston, as the self- proclaimed best children's, middle-grade, and young adult book agent in New York City, had some influence with the publisher, but Jack himself was at their mercy.

Since part of the concept of Super Rupert was the title character's fanciful imaginings of himself as a cape-clad superhero, the illustrations were kind of important to the story. He'd submitted some sketches to give his editor an idea of what he was envisioning, then crossed his fingers. When they paired him up with P.J. Blue, he'd only been able to hope for the best.

He'd been stunned the first time he opened the files on the galley of the book—at that point they were so far along in the process even if he'd detested the artwork, he wouldn't have been able to do anything about it. But the art was, in a word, perfect. It captured the whimsical, comedic, yet earnest nature of the story, and the style was accessible to the target middle grade audience.

Rupert had been a somewhat generic character, physically, when Jack first wrote him, but once P.J. drew the character, Jack couldn't imagine him any other way than with an expressive mouth, sharp nose, and wide, guileless eyes. The shock of messy dark blond hair reminded Jack of his own, and he liked the connection, since he drew on his own middle school experiences to write Rupert.

Even though he'd been pleased with how it turned out, he'd never met or even talked to P.J. Blue, except to exchange a few emails when the book was a surprise hit. He couldn't imagine Super Rupert reaching the same level of success without P.J.'s art.

As he wrote the second book, he had P.J.'s drawings pinned up on his wall, reminding him who kids would be picturing as they read. He had P.J.'s drawings of Drew as well. Rupert's friend/foe/crush was slighter of build than

Rupert, with messy dark hair long about the ears, sloped nose, and sharp chin.

The second book sold even better than the first. He'd emailed P.J. a few times in the past year since the third book came out and the fourth was supposed to have been written. He'd told P.J. about his lack of a green thumb, how he'd bought a succulent on the way home one day on a whim and it sat reproachfully on his desk, green and alive and terrifying. P.J. had told him to calm down and given him some tips for how to take care of the bundle of green cells.

Beyond that, they'd never exchanged personal information. Jack had checked out P.J.'s website. He loved the original art pieces that were showcased there, but all it said under bio was a dry paragraph about P.J.'s education and a couple of shows he'd been a part of in New York galleries. Jack had the thought once or twice that maybe if they were both in the city they should meet up, but he didn't want to ruin the magic of what they seemed to have—a strange kind of alchemy where Super Rupert bled onto the page through Jack's keyboard and P.J. filled in the gaps with the product of his pencil.

Jack halfheartedly brushed his hair and got dressed, again in shorts and a T-shirt, though this time he chose one that was slightly more fitted and less worn out and went to the kitchen. He still hadn't done any shopping, and there was nothing edible in Kingston's fridge except some Icelandic yogurt, which, while expired, wouldn't kill him. Probably.

He shut the fridge and decided his best bet was Hot Brew.

To k.james@jamesliteraryagency.com
From jonathanavery@super-rupert.com

I know you're fishing but you'll be glad to know I actually got words on the page yesterday. The place is great. Did I remember to say thanks for letting me use it?

J

To mamaavery@gmail.com
From jackrossavery@yahoo.com

The cruise sounds like an abomination against Christmas, but I'll think about it.

Love,
Your Son

To pj@pjblue-art.com
From jonathanavery@super-rupert.com

P.J.,

I'm sorry again about the delay, but I finally got the gears clicking on this thing yesterday so hopefully I'll have something for you by the end of the month. There's going to be a lot of Drew in this one, if that helps at all. Thanks for being patient.

I'm out of town for a while so I gave the plant to my neighbor. She's a much better plant parent than me.

Jonathan

Chapter 3

Pete wasn't at Hot Brew when Jack arrived, but that was okay. He'd gotten an idea for the next scene on the drive in, so he ordered a plain black coffee and a breakfast sandwich from the woman behind the counter—not Meadow— and took his same spot by the window.

He'd written a few paragraphs when the coffee and food materialized at his elbow, and he scarfed down the sandwich, letting the grease and salt work its magic. He typed faster. It was weird how quickly things had shifted. He'd been blocked by what felt like a messy pile of bricks and one day in Rosedale had seemed to open a neat path through them.

When he reached the point where he had to stand up or he'd meld with the chair, it was almost noon. He stretched his arms over his head, felt his vertebrae release one by one, and sighed. He was hungry again, and he swiveled his head to the counter to see what might be on offer for lunch.

Pete was there, fiddling with the espresso machine. He was as attractive as Jack remembered, dressed again in all black, but his hair was pulled into a little ponytail today. Jack couldn't decide if he liked it or not. He thought with a little flare of lust that if he had Pete to himself, he'd slide his hand into his hair, pull out the tie holding it back, and run his fingers through the long strands.

Pete turned around and Jack flushed, caught staring. It was really kind of a problem how attractive he found Pete. Distracting and unexpected. Wasn't he too old to get crushes?

Well, he'd been wrong about a lot of things in his life, why not this, too?

Either way, he was still staring, and Pete was smiling at him with amusement.

"Uh, hey," Jack finally said, forcing himself to act like a grownup and walk over to the counter, leaving his laptop and bag behind. Though a steady stream of customers had been in and out all morning, there were now only a handful of people inside Hot Brew.

"Hey, Jack," Pete said and damn if he didn't make Jack's name sound like a come-on. Maybe meeting someone like Pete in Rosedale was unexpected, but maybe Pete was a little bit into Jack, too.

Jack let his smile warm. "How's it going?"

"It's going." Pete leaned over the counter. He nodded at Jack's computer. "What's got you so absorbed over there?"

Jack shrugged. "Work," he said vaguely. "But it's good."

Pete looked like he was going to ask a follow up question, so Jack cut in before he could ask what kind of work. It wasn't that he was ashamed of his job, but he always felt a little pretentious explaining to strangers that he was a writer. He'd made it a habit to keep even his friends on a need-to-know basis when it came to the details of his life. "What's good for lunch here?"

Pete gave him a rundown of the menu. If he was disappointed Jack had turned the conversation back to the mundane, he didn't show it. He was, however, showing a bit of collarbone, his V-neck tee stretched even lower by the way his arms were folded against the counter and if Jack had any doubt that Pete was interested, he didn't now.

"I'll take the chicken salad," Jack decided, dragging his gaze away from the flash of bronzed skin, "and an iced coffee."

"You got it," Pete said, standing to full height.

Jack swallowed heavily. He wasn't short, but Pete had a few inches on him. Could he be any more perfect?

But how to move things beyond flirting at the counter? Asking what time he got off shift seemed clichéd beyond belief. He handed over some cash and put a generous tip in the jar. Pete noticed and winked at him. Okay. Green light.

He opened his mouth, but instead of a smooth line about meeting up later, what came out was, "You're into hanging out, maybe?" Jesus, and he called himself a writer.

Pete's laugh was surprised. Surprised at how inept Jack was, probably. "Um. Yeah. I'm into hanging out?" He said it like a question, which was fair.

Instead of banging his head against the glass pastry case, Jack tried again. "Sorry. I'm rusty. You want to hang out, with me, outside of this place sometime?"

"I thought you were only in town for a little while," Pete said.

Jack hesitated. What did that mean? Was Pete implying that Jack just wanted a brief hook up? Was he saying he was looking for something else?

"I don't know how long I'll be staying," he said finally, which was the truth. "But there's something in the water here. I've been getting a lot done, so I might stick around."

"Told you," Pete said. "All right then. I'm done here at five, we could go for a walk."

"A walk?"

"Yeah, I can show you more of the town."

"Including your place?" Jack said hopefully. He was too old to be coy.

Pete flashed white teeth. "We'll see," he said, thankfully seemingly still amused at Jack's less- than-suave approach. But then he sobered slightly. "I guess I'm rusty, too."

Jack didn't like the shadow that crossed Pete's face. Pete was so sunny—he shouldn't have anything throwing darkness his way. "Okay. So, five?"

He considered going back to Kingston's and changing but he didn't want to seem like he was trying too hard. They were going on a walk in the late afternoon humidity, not on a real date. He'd save the big guns for later.

"Five," Pete agreed.

Jack didn't see much of him the rest of the afternoon, because right after that Hot Brew was slammed with a lunch rush. Jack sat at his table protectively, eating the above-average chicken salad sandwich and getting his caffeine buzz back on. He would have felt guilty about hogging a table for the entire day, but the lunch crowd mostly seemed to be folks who were getting something to take back to their offices. Jack smiled. He liked his makeshift office at Hot Brew.

He wrote a little bit more, paid some bills, and caught up on his email. P.J. hadn't written back, not that he was obligated to. The feeling of procrastination wasn't quite so intense now that he was pretty sure where the story was going. He was burned out on writing for the day, but he wasn't dreading tomorrow. He knew now that the words would come.

Pete was busy, but a couple of times when

it was slow, Jack saw him leaning against the counter again, writing in a slim black notebook that he'd shove into the back pocket of his jeans when a customer came in. What was he writing in there? Coffee recipes? Bad poetry? It was probably something like lists of things that needed to be restocked, which reminded Jack of his own need to visit a grocery store. He couldn't eat three meals a day at Hot Brew. Well he could, but he probably shouldn't. The Italian place last night had been great— wholesome and hearty and the really good house red hadn't hurt the experience, either. He wondered if Pete would come with him next time.

Speaking of which, it was nearly five. Jack had managed to use up the entire afternoon, and he felt strangely nervous now. He went to the restroom, splashed some water on his face. He stroked his weirdly ginger-colored five o'clock shadow, considering his hair was light brown. He probably should have taken the time to shave that morning. Oh well. He shouldered his bag and nearly ran into Pete in the hallway outside the restroom.

"Oh, hey, sorry," Pete said, taking the words out of Jack's mouth. "You ready? Give me a minute."

"Of course. I'll wait out front."

Meadow was behind the counter, and she gave Jack a knowing look when he hovered by the pastry case, trying to look like he belonged.

"You're back."

"Yep." Jack nodded, smiling. "You guys hooked me."

"I bet we did. Well, have fun," Meadow said in a teasing tone. "And see you soon."

Jack would have been annoyed, but since he was indeed hoping to have fun with Pete, he couldn't really complain.

The next minute Pete appeared, sans apron, hair out of the ponytail, and steered him out of the store with a wave to Meadow.

The late afternoon sun filtered through a layer of gray clouds, increasing the humidity, and it felt like an oven after the air-conditioned interior of Hot Brew. Jack felt sweat pop out on his forehead almost immediately. Pete didn't seem bothered, just started walking up the street, his long legs eating up the sidewalk.

"So this is the downtown strip, but there are some great shops down the side streets, too," he said, pointing out a few, including a promising-looking bookstore. "And a good bar over there." He gestured to a tiny Irish pub sandwiched between a hipster tattoo parlor and a clothing store. "Happy hour half price pints."

"Good to know," Jack said.

"The Art Center's at the top of the hill there, and my place is on the other side. You up for the walk?"

"You don't have a car?"

"Nah. It's a pain sometimes but I get by with rides from friends and there's a bus that goes to the big box stores by the highway. You have a car?"

"Not in the city, but I have a rental right now. Where I'm staying is too far to walk here."

"Oh yeah, when I got here, I was staying at a friend's and I had a rental, too, otherwise I would have been stuck in the country."

"Nice friend," Jack commented.

"The best. He saved me by inviting me here." There was that shadow again. Jack found himself wanting the full story, but before he could ask, Pete went on. "Rosedale really is cool. If you have time, you should come to the Arts Center tomorrow night. They're having a community dinner and an open house to showcase some of their summer students' works."

"Will you be there?" Jack asked.

"Yeah." Pete's smile showed his dimples.

"I'll try to make it."

They walked on, and the shops gave way to old houses. Some of them had white signs proclaiming the year of their construction, most seeming to be from the early 1800s.

"As a bona fide city person, I agree with you that Rosedale is cool. Can't imagine there's much of a dating scene, though," Jack said casually. "Unless you do the Internet thing." He was fishing, looking for confirmation that Pete was at least into guys, but he wasn't expecting Pete's answer.

"That's another plus, in my book," Pete said with a shade of bitterness.

Things were becoming clearer. Pete had needed to leave the city, he'd found refuge in this one-horse town, and he'd been giving Jack mixed signals since he'd first walked through the door at Hot Brew.

"Bad breakup?" Jack guessed.

Pete turned his head sharply to look at him. "Yeah. Really fucking bad, actually. Is it that obvious?"

They'd passed the historic houses and found themselves in a small, old graveyard ringed by spindly evergreens. They stopped in the shade and Jack immediately felt cooler.

"One of the only reasons I can think of why a guy like you wouldn't be looking to hook up."

"A guy like me?" Pete said, with a sort of

hopeful smile on his face. Better than the bitterness.

Jack hedged. "Young, um, tall."

Pete rounded his shoulders as if at the reminder of his height. "There's a trail through the community woods we can take if you want."

"Wait." Jack touched Pete's elbow. Pete's warmth bled into his fingers before he let go. The brief touch made him certain that he wanted his hands on every inch of Pete's body before long. "Sorry, I mean you're gorgeous. I can't imagine everyone in town doesn't want a chance with you."

"Gorgeous?" Pete looked at him skeptically.

"Yeah, you've gotta know you're fucking gorgeous, Pete," Jack said. When Pete didn't say anything, he wondered if he'd read this all wrong. "Is it okay that I think that?"

Pete walked toward the trailhead leading into the woods. "Yeah. Of course. It's just been a while since I've let myself think about—" He stopped and looked Jack up and down. Jack let him look, skin prickling under the sweep of Pete's gaze. "And I didn't exactly expect to meet someone like you in Rosedale."

"Someone like me?" Jack asked, in echo of Pete's line from before.

"Rosedale is great, but I think you brought up the average attractiveness level by about ten points just by walking into town."

Jack huffed out a laugh. "You're really too kind. See me after a shave and some hair gel. Maybe in something other than a T-shirt."

"Hope I get to," Pete said.

That was the best thing Jack had heard all day.

They walked for about a quarter mile and came to the beginning of a loop.

"You can take this all the way around the woods, if you want, and it brings you right back here." Pete spoke with his hands, pointing at the sign and the trail markers. "But we don't have to do it today. I'm kind of getting hungry for dinner."

"Same. I'd ask you back to where I'm

staying but there is literally no food there. I haven't gone grocery shopping yet."

"You like tacos? There's a good little place back in town."

"Who doesn't like tacos?"

Pete laughed at that, even though it wasn't particularly funny. "My ex, for one."

"Well, there's a red flag if I ever heard one." Jack wondered if he'd ever get to hear the story of the bad breakup, or if he'd ever get a chance to punch whoever hurt Pete in the face. Euphemistically. He'd never been in a fight in his life, and it wasn't exactly on his bucket list. Maybe he could write the bastard into the Super Rupert books as a villain.

Pete laughed again, and this time it sounded lighter. "Shoulda listened to my instincts the first time he turned down carnitas."

"Totally." Jack internally pumped his fist at the pronoun of Pete's ex, while his stomach growled at the suggestion of food. "Let's do it."

They hiked back the way they came. Jack

was feeling hot and gross by the time they made it back to town. Pete was glowing, tanned skin burnished with a sheen of sweat. The taco place was busy, so they got takeout and carried it to a bench on the main drag where they could watch the streetlights come on. Down the street, Hot Brew's neon open sign glowed blue.

Jack watched with wide eyes as Pete inhaled his first taco in two bites. The food was great, but it was more fun to focus on Pete, his big hands dwarfing the tacos.

"You have an apartment?" Jack asked.

Pete explained that he rented a room in a house, and Jack realized that meant not a lot of privacy. He was living in a borrowed house, but unless Kingston dropped by unannounced, they could be safely alone there. If they got to that point.

He'd had his share of brief hookups in the day, but he was getting a little old for one and done relationships. Or maybe there was something about Pete that made him want to take his time. Maybe the shadows in Pete's eyes made him not want to be something he regretted.

He was about to suggest they set a date for their, well, date, but the sky, which had steadily been growing darker, suddenly started pelting water at them. The rain wasn't cold, but it was hard, and they leapt off the bench. Pete turned his face to the sky and laughed. Jack appreciated the sight for a second before he balled up the paper his tacos had come in and tossed it in a nearby garbage can.

"Come on," he said. "My car's around the corner. I'll give you a ride."

Chapter 4

Jack's black sedan was the nicest rental Pete had ever seen. It had a leather interior and all the bells and whistles. Pete felt big and messy, like a wet dog, as he settled into the passenger seat.

"Sweet car," he said.

"Thanks. It drives well," Jack said offhandedly. "Where to?"

Pete directed him to Carol's. The drive took all of four minutes, but Pete did appreciate not having his sneakers completely soaked by the time he got home. Carol's hatchback was in the driveway, and even though Jack looked improbably cute with a smear of sour cream on his whiskery cheek, Pete decided he wasn't going to kiss him.

They'd only met yesterday, and even if he'd grown strangely comfortable with Jack after such a short period of time, Pete couldn't trust himself to make good decisions when it came to men. He'd taken a hard pass on anything having to do with physical relationships after he left the city. He wanted to see where things with Jack might go, but he was gun shy about making any move that would turn out to be a mistake.

He didn't lean across the center console and kiss the handsome man in the driver's seat. He didn't even invite Jack inside. But he said, "I'm off tomorrow, but maybe I'll see you at the Art Center open house? I can text you the address."

"Oh yeah?" Jack said. "Is that your way of asking for my number?"

Mistakes like that. Pete had been slowly

making friends in Rosedale; he'd forgotten what it was like to talk to someone who had the possibility of ending up in his bed. He rolled his eyes defensively. "Yeah, I guess so. You want mine first?"

Instead of making fun of him, Jack just said, "Absolutely," and got out his phone.

Pete reeled off his number and Jack typed it in. A second later, Pete's phone buzzed in his pocket.

"Now you have mine."

Jack's smile was unfair. How was Pete supposed to stick to his resolution and get out of the car without tasting those sinfully sculpted lips? But he wrenched his gaze away, reminding himself that Kurt's smile had been charming once, too.

The rain was still coming down hard.

"Drive safe. See you tomorrow," Pete said. He got out and slammed the door before Jack could say—or do—anything else.

He let himself in, hollered a hello to Carol

who was puttering in the kitchen. He went to his room and stripped off his damp clothes, the scent of his own sweat from their walk and the humidity and a day of work turning him on a little. He wondered what Jack smelled like. He licked his lips thinking about Jack's smooth, freckle-dotted skin.

When he said he hoped he'd find out what Jack looked like when he cleaned up a bit, he wasn't lying. He wanted that, more than he knew what to do with. But it was a little fast considering he was going from full abstention to wanting to jump Jack's bones in the span of a day.

Two days, he reasoned as he stepped under the spray of the shower and sluiced off. He soaped up and ignored his thickening cock. He didn't need to get on top of Jack, and he didn't need to jerk off, either. He needed to work.

He'd gotten an email back from Jonathan and even if he hadn't said much, he had told him that Drew would be in the upcoming book. Pete could practice drawing him. It was something tangible he could put himself to work on. And it was welcome news, besides. Drew was fun to draw, and an interesting character. He'd started out as an antagonist, had become an ally of Rupert's, and along the way he and Rupert had explored thirteen-year-old flirting which was both hilarious and sweet and occasionally cringe-worthy. Jonathan had written Rupert as somewhat oblivious about exactly how much Drew liked him back, but Pete, in his many close readings of the text, could tell Drew was into Rupert, he just kept things close to the vest. Pete couldn't wait to see where Jonathan was taking the story in the next installment.

He threw on some boxers and a T-shirt and fired up his computer. The drawing tablet had taken time to learn, but using it felt as natural as pencil on paper now, the stylus an extension of his hand. Everything he drew went into a program to be manipulated, edited, layered, and polished until he had exactly what he wanted. Or as close to exactly what he wanted as any artist could achieve.

Drawing soothed the rough edges of his emotions from his day and from the effort of getting to know someone new, someone who kept him on his toes and ignited sparks inside of him that he'd thought might never get lit again.

He drew until his hand cramped, then he saved everything and shut off the light, dreaming of green eyes and messy hair, stubble-rough kisses and getting caught in a downpour of warm summer rain.

"He's not here," Meadow said, knowing smile back on her face the next morning when Jack walked into Hot Brew.

"I know," Jack said, then bit his tongue

when her smirk deepened. "Whatever. Can I get a coffee and a breakfast sandwich, please?"

She rang him up with a minimum of snark and he took his usual seat. While he waited for his food, he checked his email. There was a new message from P.J., time stamped around midnight.

To jonathanavery@super-rupert.com
From pj@pjblue-art.com

Just a few things I worked on tonight.
What do you think?

P.J.

Strictly speaking, Jack wasn't supposed to have input on the artwork, but since the Super Rupert books sold well and he had a good relationship with his publisher, there wasn't anything wrong with looking at some of P.J.'s art.

He opened the attachment eagerly, and smiled at the familiar face of Drew in a variety of expressions and poses. He paused on the last one. Drew was sitting at a table, a book open in front of him, but he wasn't reading it. He was looking at Rupert, a less detailed sketch of the main character on the other side of the page. Drew's expression was a little bit longing, a little bit fearful. It was as if Drew knew he wanted Rupert and he was scared by the knowledge.

Having your first crush on a boy was kind of like that.

His first was on Nate Fishman and it had been way before eighth grade, but it had still been slightly terrifying to realize the person he most wanted to see every day wasn't safe, predictable Gabby McBride, but quirky, funny Nate with his dark eyes and curly hair. Alas, even Nate had wanted Gabby. Jack was pretty sure they'd even dated for a while in high school.

That's why fiction was better than real life

sometimes. Okay, a lot of times. Rupert and Drew were clueless middle schoolers, but he could give them a happier ending than a lot of the kids reading the book might have for a long while.

He saved the picture of Drew looking at Rupert to his desktop and thanked Meadow when she brought his order over. He worked all morning, only stopping when his phone buzzed with a text from Pete. He'd been hoping for a little bit more than an address and a time—6PM—but he'd take it.

He'd almost thought Pete might kiss him last night in the car when they were steaming up the inside from being wet, unfortunately not for any other reason. But then he went home and saw the smear of sour cream on his face, and he'd been glad their first kiss hadn't happened when he was covered in food like a child.

Jack saved the morning's work and ordered a sandwich to go. He wanted to check out a few of the shops on the main drag before he went back to Kingston's. Even if this was a casual friend hang out thing and not a proper date, he was determined to look put together.

Tucking the sandwich in his bag for later, he set off. Last night's storm had broken the humidity and even though it was still hot, the summer sun was less oppressive in the crystal blue sky. He'd surveyed the clothes he'd brought up from the city with him and had to question what he'd been thinking when he packed six T-shirts, three pairs of shorts, and a pair of joggers. He supposed he hadn't expected to want to woo a handsome barista, but still, he couldn't have thrown in one button-down or even a Hawaiian shirt for god's sake?

First stop was a local men's clothing store. He found a couple of short sleeved button downs, one a crisp white and the other a dark green. He also grabbed a pair of swim shorts and a pair of flip flops. Pete had mentioned that the only pool in town was at the local tennis club which was private but where you could get day passes. Pants were a little more difficult, but Jack found a pair of dark washed jeans that fit. He was pleasantly surprised at the register. Buying a bagful of clothes in Manhattan would have set him back three times the amount the clerk rang up on his credit card.

He ate his sandwich on the same bench where he and Pete ate their tacos yesterday and watched the foot traffic. Belatedly, he realized today was Friday. It seemed busier in town, and he wondered how much of Rosedale's economy relied on tourism or weekend residents who came up from the city.

Kingston had owned his place for a few years as a retreat to get his head screwed on straight when the city got to be too much. Jack had never seen the point in the expense and trouble of keeping up two places to live, but he had to admit the town was growing on him. And it wasn't just because of Pete. Everyone was friendly and the food was as good as anything he'd had in the city. He was enjoying having a car. He'd felt like a hero being able to offer Pete a ride home in the rain the night before, even if the drive had been about the length of a pop song.

Before he went home to change, he went to the bookstore Pete had pointed out to him on their tour. Like any writer, he had a weakness for books. It was a small shop but had a nice selection of volumes neatly arranged on blond wood shelves. He nodded to the clerk behind the counter and browsed the nonfiction section. When he was writing he found it difficult to read fiction, especially middle grade fiction, since he made inevitable, unhelpful comparisons to his own work. Still, he couldn't help compulsively checking the young readers area for his own books. To his delight, they had all three Super Rupert books prominently displayed. He grabbed one off the shelf.

Would it be cringe to offer to sign it? He glanced at the clerk who smiled at him.

"That's a great series," she said. "Looking for a gift?"

"No, just browsing. But I'm glad you like this. I wrote it," he said, only a tiny bit self-consciously.

Her eyes widened. "You're Jonathan Avery?"

"Yeah." He smiled and waved the book at her. "Can I sign this, or would that decrease its value?"

She scoffed and held up a permanent marker. "You have to sign them all, if you have time."

"Sure," Jack agreed. He opened the book to the title page and looked down in puzzlement. "Looks like you already have someone's autograph." The next second the squiggly signature resolved itself into meaning. "P.J. Blue" it read, with a little smiley face in P.J.'s trademark style.

"Oh yeah, the illustrator lives here in Rosedale. He signed these a little bit ago.

We've sold a few since then, though. I should probably put in another order."

"Wait, what? P.J. Blue lives in Rosedale?"

"Yeah, I've never met him, but my boss mentioned it. I guess he came in one day, just like you, and she got him to sign them all."

Jack signed the small stack of books on autopilot, positioning his name on the same line as P.J.'s, careful not to overlap. What the hell? In what universe did it make any sense whatsoever that the illustrator of the Super Rupert books lived in Rosedale of all places? For one thing wouldn't P.J. have mentioned it? Except they didn't talk about personal things, not really. Jack's houseplants didn't count. Jack didn't even know what P.J. Blue looked like. He could have been his next-door neighbor for all Jack knew.

He handed the marker back to the clerk, learned her name was Melissa, and offered to come back and sign more if he was still in town when the next shipment came in.

"Is the fourth book coming out soon?" she

asked eagerly. "My younger brother is a huge fan."

"It's scheduled to come out before the holidays," Jack said, still trying to process.

"Awesome, well, great to meet you," Melissa said enthusiastically.

Jack had a hard time keeping his mind on book browsing, but he found a biography of Margaret Wise Brown he'd been meaning to read, and he bought it, slipping it into the bag next to his clothes purchases. He drove home, well, not home, Kingston's home. Kingston. Wait. Kingston might know what the deal with P.J. was. Or maybe Jack could simply email P.J. directly and clear the whole thing up.

When he checked the clock though, he cursed. He didn't have time to unravel the mystery of P.J. Blue. He had to get ready to see Pete. Anticipation trumped confusion. He'd missed seeing Pete's face at the coffee shop today. He showered and shaved, stole some expensive aftershave he found in Kingston's medicine cabinet. He spent way too long trying to tame his hair into something that looked halfway on purpose, tore the tags off the green shirt, changed to the white one, then put the green one back on.

He grabbed his keys, took a steadying breath. Maybe by the end of the day he'd have a kiss to show for all his hard work.

Chapter 5

"Can you check if Nick needs more name tags, Pete darling?" Che, the Art Center director, asked as they fluttered around the reception space. The open house had begun and streams of people were coming in and out of the main gallery, while dinner was being set up on the interior courtyard of the big white building at the top of Rosedale Hill.

"On it," Pete said, checking his phone for the fifth time in as many minutes. It was just now six, so Jack wasn't late yet. Not that he had to be perfectly on time. Pete wasn't a stickler about things like that. He was just half worried Jack wouldn't show at all, and the tiny baby step he'd made toward opening himself up to someone again would be crushed and he'd be back to square one.

But when he got to the entrance and confirmed that Nick, another Art Center volunteer, had plenty of name tags, he saw Jack. He'd already received a name tag; the white rectangle stood out on his dark green shirt, his name written in neat block letters. The shirt made Jack's eyes pop like bottle glass held up to the sun. He'd shaved and dark jeans completed the look. He looked mouth wateringly good. The fact that he'd made an effort to look nice for Pete—he couldn't help the hot blush on his cheeks, which was mortifying. He was twenty-eight, not eighteen. But then, he'd never had anyone as hot as Jack make an effort for him at eighteen.

He walked over, and Jack's face lit up. It was hard not to touch him, but they were barely friends. A hug would have been weird.

Right? Still, it was rather noisy in the crowded entryway, so Pete took the opportunity to slide in as close as he dared.

"Hello." Jack smelled good. Like, really good, and Pete's blush found new fuel. Suddenly, he felt every day of celibacy of the last six-plus-months like a fire at the base of his spine that made him want to drag Jack to a dark corner and beg him to put an end to his abstinence right that very minute.

But he kept an appropriate distance between them, and Jack said hello back and then asked if there was a bar. Pete was able to calm down enough to take him to the back where Tyrone was selling cans of local brews and seltzers. Pete got a water, Jack got a pilsner, and they made small talk while they waited in line for dinner. Pete's stomach was nervy, but he knew he'd regret it if he didn't have food.

"After we eat, I'll show you the gallery," Pete said. "There are some amazing pieces up right now. The summer program has been producing some great stuff. One of my students from the spring session has a solo show going up in a few weeks, and she has some pieces here, too."

"You're a teacher?" Jack asked, surprised.

Pete had purposefully kept the details of his life vague as they'd gotten to know each other. There was no reason to go overboard right away. He'd learned that the hard way with Kurt. But Jack wasn't Kurt. He wasn't going to take every nugget of Pete's life and find a way to twist it into something that benefited him.

"Drawing, yeah. I started off volunteering when I first got here, then they offered me a couple of evening classes. I really love it. My students often inspire my own work."

"That's so cool. You draw? Can I see your stuff?"

Pete rubbed the back of his neck. No matter how established he got, he still got nervous about showing his work to people whose opinion he cared about. "Sure. I guess."

They shuffled forward in line, sparing Pete the need of actually having to do it.

Dinner was buffet-style, the food contributed by local restaurants. Pete watched Jack take some salad and a small piece of fish. He seemed to look longingly at the stack of sourdough rolls but didn't put one on his plate.

"No bread?" Pete asked, grabbing a roll for himself to go with his portion of lasagna and smaller pile of green salad.

"I've been indulging too much at Hot Brew," Jack said ruefully. He patted his belly, which made Pete want to reach out and feel the curves of Jack's flesh for himself. "I need to decrease my carbs and take a few more walks in those woods you showed me."

"Well, I'm happy to walk with you anytime," Pete said, "but I think you look great."

"Yeah?" Jack's smile was sweet and boyish, and Pete wondered how anyone so patently attractive was still on the market. He reminded himself he didn't really know Jack at all. He probably had some deep dark secret that made him a disaster waiting to happen.

But what little he knew of Jack, he liked, so maybe it would be worth it.

"Yeah," he said, maneuvering his plate so he could take a roll-up of silverware. He led them to the end of a picnic table, nodding at a small group on the other end of the table. Jack slid into the seat across from him and they started to eat and talk about the local food scene. Jack was impressed, even coming from the city.

"You should try the Thai place," Pete suggested. He broke his roll in two and offered Jack the other half. "And Stacy's bread is amazing. She sells it at the Sunday farmer's market."

Jack looked from the bread to Pete. "Wait, is this the secret you've been keeping?"

"What?" Pete was confused. He had a few secrets, but none were bread related.

"Does the bread make everyone fall in love with Rosedale? Is that why people come here from New York and never leave? Some kind of pod people thing?"

There was a twinkle in Jack's eyes and Pete laughed. "If it is, man, I don't want to know. I like it here."

"That's what they want." But he took the bread and bit into it with relish. "Fuck, that's good."

Watching Jack eat carbs was dangerous. His pink lips wrapped around the hunk of bread and Pete couldn't help imagining those lips doing things to certain parts of his anatomy.

He forced himself to look away, ate half his lasagna without tasting it. Was he in trouble here? Jack was only in town for a little while. Maybe that's what Pete needed—something simple and with a built-in expiration date to get his feet wet and finish getting over Kurt for good. What was that saying—the best way to get over someone was to get under someone else? He hadn't wanted anyone in so long, and now Jack had blown into his life and he hadn't been able to stop thinking about much else beside the way he'd taste, or what sounds he'd make if Pete took him to one of the empty classrooms, crowded him against a wall, touched him in all the places he'd been craving getting his hands on.

He blinked and realized Jack was asking him a question. "—farmer's market?"

"Say that again, sorry," Pete said. He needed to get his head together.

"I was wondering where the farmer's market is. You okay? You seem like you're somewhere else." Jack didn't sound offended, just curious.

Pete didn't quite know how to tell him that his mind had been wandering off to a dark corner with Jack himself. He cleared his throat and pushed his empty plate away. "They close the side street near Hot Brew Sunday mornings. Ten to one, I think?"

"Maybe I'll check it out this weekend. You working?"

Pete mentally reviewed his schedule. "Not

Sunday. We could go for that walk before it gets hot and then hit up the market."

Jack smiled happily. "Sounds great."

"You want to walk around? I'd like to show off my students' work." He waited while Jack finished his meal, and they cleared their plates, agreeing to come back for dessert. Jack would make an excellent dessert, Pete mused as they went back into the main gallery.

Jack stayed closed to his side, letting their arms brush occasionally. They paused in front of a still life one of his favorite students had drawn of her cat sleeping on a stack of comic books.

"This is so detailed—it looks like a black and white photograph," Jack said.

"We always start with pencil drawings, then move onto color, but Nancee really got into the monochromatic palette," Pete explained.

"Hey—I know her," Jack said, nodding to a woman on the other side of the room. "Melissa. She works in the bookstore. I dropped in there today."

"Oh yeah," Pete said. He recognized her but didn't think they'd ever met. He'd met the woman she was with though, Trish. "That's the owner with her."

"Nice bookstore," Jack said. Melissa noticed him and waved. She said something to Trish and the two women walked over.

"Hello," Melissa said to Jack. "You're turning up everywhere today."

"Small town," Jack said with a friendly smile.

"This is my boss, Trish."

Trish smiled at them, and Pete gave a little wave. They didn't know each other well, but it was always a good idea to keep on a bookstore owner's good side.

"Thanks for signing those books," Trish said.

"You're welcome," Pete said, at the same time Jack said, "Anytime."

They looked at each other, but before either one could voice the question, Trish spoke again. "You know, since you're both in town, it would be amazing to have some kind of event at the shop. We could do a reading and signing or even an art project for the kids? Would you two be up for something like that?"

Pete was confused. Trish knew he illustrated the Super Rupert books—they'd talked about it when he'd stopped into the store one day and she'd asked him to sign what they had in stock. But why was she talking as if he and Jack were a package deal?

Jack's brow wrinkled. "Since both of us…?" He looked at Pete.

"Let me know, and we'll set something up. Really nice to meet you, Jonathan," Trish said, smiling warmly at Jack. "Do you go by Jonathan, or do you have an alter ego like Pete here?"

"Call me Jack." He was still looking at Pete, eyes narrowed, as if he was trying to figure something out.

Pete knew how he felt. He was trying to put the pieces together, but what he was coming up with seemed completely ludicrous.

"Well, we all adore Super Rupert, so we can't wait for the next book," Trish said. "See you later, I hope. Bye Jack. Bye Pete."

"Nice to meet you," Jack said faintly, his gaze never leaving Pete.

Pete vaguely registered Melissa and Trish leaving to resume their tour of the gallery walls. "What the fuck was that?"

Chapter 6

"I think I might have figured it out," Jack said. He walked past Pete and to the next wall of art where a piece Pete had worked on earlier in the summer was displayed. It was a line drawing in his usual style, an active scene of locals enjoying the summer carnival the town had sponsored around Memorial Day.

Pete followed him over, startling when Jack turned around quickly and said, "This is your work." He made it sound like an accusation.

Pete nodded. "So?"

"I can't believe this," Jack said, looking

back at the drawing. "You told me your name was Pete."

The harsh tone made Pete's stomach dip. It reminded him of Kurt, who had not only bled Pete's bank account dry, used his name to open a line of credit, and cheated on him with one of his so-called friends, had the gall to turn it all around on Pete when he'd been caught, accusing Pete of being withholding and frigid and so fixated on his art that he'd been forced to look for companionship elsewhere. Pete shuddered, pushing away the sight of Kurt's face, livid with rage when Pete had finally summoned the courage to end their toxic relationship.

"It is," he said haltingly. "Why?"

Jack pointed to the squiggle where he'd signed his art. "You're P.J. Blue," he said, sounding dazed.

"It's not a secret. Not really," Pete said, feeling defensive. "I use a different name to sell and market my art. It's not uncommon."

"Neither is publishing under another

name." He met Pete's gaze head on. "I'm Jonathan Avery."

"Jonathan Avery," he repeated. That tracked with what Trish said—he just hadn't wanted to hear it. He hadn't wanted to be right —or wrong—about Jack. Of course he couldn't have nice things, he thought bitterly. Of course the only guy he'd taken an interest in since Kurt would turn out to be someone he could never have.

"You're Jonathan Avery, the author?" a woman who had been looking at a nearby painting said to Jack. "My kids love your books." She looked at Pete, then at his drawing. "No way, and you're the illustrator? This is so cool. Are you two working together on a new book?"

"No," they said simultaneously. Pete glared at Jack, who scowled back.

The woman's laugh was slightly awkward. "Okay. Well. Um. Nice to meet you," she said before walking away.

"Damn," Jack said. "We should have been nicer to her."

"We should probably talk." Pete couldn't figure out where to start with all his questions and the middle of the crowded gallery wasn't the place for the breakdown he felt he was entitled to. "Come with me."

He made sure Jack was following him, then went to the exit that led to the classrooms. It was quieter back there, and he opened the door to a room he'd known would be empty—the drawing studio. It smelled comfortingly of pencil shavings and eraser rubber.

He looked at Jack, whose expression was unreadable. Even in the dim light of the darkened classroom, his eyes were the clearest green Pete had ever seen. He launched into his first question. "How are you Jonathan Avery—I mean, what are the odds? And how did we not know?"

"I don't know. This is unbelievable," Jack said, starting to pace. "I went to the bookstore today and saw they had some Super Rupert books. That woman—Melissa—asked me to sign them and they'd already been signed by P.J. Blue—I mean, by you. I was so confused. But it never occurred to me that you—"

Suddenly, Jack stopped moving and a smile broke out on his handsome face. In an instant, Pete found himself crushed against Jack in a bear hug that lasted several seconds before Jack let him go.

"Pete—I mean P.J.—it's so amazing to meet you. Or know you. Or whatever. This is confusing. But incredible. Your art is fantastic. I owe you so much, I mean, your art makes the Super Rupert books really special. I think you know that, but yeah. Thanks, man."

Pete tried to come up with a combination of words that would in some way acknowledge the enormity of what Jack had just said but failed miserably. "You're welcome?"

Jack laughed. "Tell me everything. How did you end up here? Why the P.J.? What's with the barista job? Seriously, I have so many questions."

Pete blinked. "That's for sure." He was still trying to process Jack calling his art fantastic. Sure, he'd gotten a nice note from Jonathan—Jack—after the first book started selling well, but their contact since then had been decidedly businesslike, except for when Pete had let his better nature take over in emails and injected a few personal notes here and there.

"Come on, spill," Jack said, making an impatient motion with his hand.

"Wait, I have questions of my own. How did you end up in Rosedale? Why did you decide to publish under a different name? And is that what you've been working on every day in Hot Brew—the new Super Rupert?"

"Okay, fair enough. In reverse order, yes, I've been working on my hideously overdue manuscript since I got here with the help of your amazing coffee. My book agent suggested I publish under my full name, but I've always gone by Jack in my personal life. And speaking of my agent, that's how I ended up in Rosedale. I'm staying at Kingston's house."

"Kingston James is your agent?" Things were suddenly getting clearer. Kingston was the invisible thread that linked them together.

"How do you know him? He doesn't represent illustrators."

"He's not my agent, but I've known him for years. He's a friend. He's the one who gave my portfolio to the publisher. When I needed to get out of the city, he offered me his place—wait, that's where you're staying now? The house on Bramble Street?" Pete laughed in amazement.

This was such a small world.

"Yep," Jack confirmed. "I had no idea you knew Kingston."

"Weird."

"Well, whatever led us here, I'm really glad we met," Jack said quietly.

It should have been reassuring that Jack seemed so fine with everything, but Pete wasn't sure what this meant for them. "I'm glad we met, too. I think."

Jack raised his eyebrows. "You think?"

"I mean, of course I am. Your words inspired me to do the work I'm most proud of in my career so far. I love Super Rupert. I think you're brilliant. But—"

"We make a good team," Jack interrupted.

"Right. A good professional team. We're essentially coworkers. Don't you see what that means?"

Jack's face slowly fell. "Oh. Wait. You think that just because Jonathan Avery and P.J. Blue work together, Jack and Pete can't date?"

Pete put aside the flutter in his belly at Jack implying he wanted to date him. "You make us sound like four different people, but we're only two. Two guys who have to keep working together, maybe for a while to come."

"We can be grownups about this. Finding out you're P.J. Blue—Pete, I have to be honest, it doesn't make me like you less. It makes me think you're even more awesome than I already did." Jack's voice was deep and sincere.

Pete winced. He couldn't lie and say he didn't get a rush from knowing Jack felt like that about him, but it was simply not possible. "I'm sorry. I can't work with you and be involved...emotionally."

Jack was quiet. He looked at the floor. Pete was worried he might ask him why, and that was a subject he didn't want to get into with Jack now. Maybe not ever.

But Jack didn't ask, just glanced back up and said, "So, what, we can't even be friends?"

Pete blew out a breath. Friends shouldn't be too much to ask. Problem was, he didn't know if he could be friends with someone he was so attracted to. Just because he'd discovered Jack was off-limits didn't mean he was suddenly repulsive. Honestly, he'd never looked better here in the half light of the drawing studio, his long golden brown lashes casting shadows over his lightly freckled cheeks, his mouth pursed unhappily. He looked like a moody angel, and Pete had the very strong urge to draw him. He felt like he could spend a lifetime trying to capture the planes and angles of Jack's face, attempting to reproduce the exact angle of the divot in his upper lip, and he'd never get tired of the subject.

But he wasn't going to get that chance.

"I'd like to be your friend," he answered eventually. "I mean, you aren't going to be in Rosedale that long, anyway, right? There's no point in us avoiding each other. Maybe we could even bounce some ideas off each other if that would be helpful. But anything else—it's not a good idea."

Jack looked like he wanted to argue, but he bit his lip and nodded. "Okay. You're right. I'm not even going to be here that much longer. The book is coming along quickly now. Might only be a few more days."

Pete flinched. Only a few more days to see Jack before he went back to the city? Still, what if he'd let himself be dragged in further by those beautiful eyes, had fallen even harder for Jack? It was better this way.

That's what he told himself, anyway.

Chapter 7

Jack woke up the morning after the Art Center dinner feeling as if a huge weight was pressing him down into the bed. And it wasn't the sexy, muscular weight of a handsome man who'd wake him up with bristly kisses. It was the weight of disappointment, the knowledge that Pete wanted barely anything to do with him now that he knew they were both responsible for the top selling middle grade series of the last couple of years.

He got that it was complicated. Once he'd gotten over his initial shock that not only did

P.J. Blue live in Rosedale, but his alter ego was the cute guy Jack had been crushing on at Hot Brew, he'd been counting his blessings. Pete was P.J. and that was awesome, because Jack thought Pete was cute and funny and smart, and he thought P.J. was talented and creative and he respected the hell out of him. To find out they were one and the same seemed on the surface like the best kind of serendipity.

But he saw Pete's point. What if they started something physical and it didn't work out—they'd still have to work on Super Rupert together. There was a reason publishers didn't usually encourage writers and illustrators to interact. It didn't do anybody any good if they were involved in any capacity other than as author and illustrator.

But that was all theoretical. In reality, Pete was smoking hot and Jack liked him so, so much.

Except apparently Pete didn't like him back, or not enough to risk it. And Jack was going to have to accept the meager crumbs

Pete was allowing him—to be on friendly terms while he was still in Rosedale—and pretend he was okay with it.

He heaved out of bed, trying to shake off his mood. He'd been so full of excitement about getting to know Pete, so full of curiosity about the Art Center and the bookstore and had been beginning to fall in love with Rosedale, the way everyone said he would. He was afraid he'd also started to fall in love with Pete. He didn't know what to do with those feelings swirling around inside him, no way to get out, like a butterfly trapped in a greenhouse.

He still had not gone grocery shopping, so even though he wasn't even sure if Pete would be at Hot Brew that morning, he made his way downtown and parked in his usual spot in an all-day space around the corner from the coffee shop.

Meadow was working, but he didn't see Pete. He ordered what was becoming his usual, and she brought it to him without a word. The coffee burned through the fog in his brain like the sun burning through the morning mist hanging over Rosedale's community woods.

But still, as he opened his document and looked at where he'd left off the previous day, he sighed, a familiar paralysis taking over. The flush of serotonin over meeting Pete, of seeing the possibilities there, had broken his block on the manuscript, but now as he contemplated Rupert's next move, he was at a loss. He needed Rupert and Drew to get closer, to cross into uncharted territory. Rupert was ready. But was Drew?

He clicked away from the document and on the drawing P.J.—Pete—P.J. had sent him just a couple of days earlier. Drew's longing glance at Rupert. Dammit, Drew was ready.

Why wasn't Pete?

He let his frustration spill through his fingers and started typing. He struggled through half a scene before he looked up and saw Pete waiting on someone at the counter.

He looked subdued today. His uniform of black seemed funereal rather than artsy. He barely smiled as he took the customer's order, and he didn't look in Jack's direction. Was he ignoring him on purpose?

Jack shut his computer with a click and got in line. The woman Pete had been waiting on moved to the side and started looking at her phone and Jack stepped into her place.

"Hi." His voice was gravel rough, as if he hadn't used it in a while. He'd practically grunted his order at Meadow that morning, so he supposed he hadn't. After they'd left the empty classroom the previous night where all of Jack's hopes had been crushed, Pete had made an excuse and taken off before he'd even shown Jack the rest of the art show as he'd promised.

Jack didn't know how to do this, how to be friends with someone he was so exasperated with, and who he wanted so badly.

"Hey," Pete said with barely any inflection in his voice. "Can I get you something?"

"I already ate," Jack said. "Are you okay?"

Meadow appeared from the back and handed the woman on her phone a paper to-go bag. She glanced between the two of them curiously but said nothing and went to clean the milk frother.

"I'm fine, yeah. Thanks," Pete said, but he didn't sound very convincing. Jack saw the shadow in his eyes and hated that he was somehow responsible for putting it there.

"Dammit, Pete, this isn't our fault," he said, his frustration from earlier boiling over. "I get why it's not a good idea, but I hate that things are weird between us now."

Pete sighed, ran a hand through his hair, which was hanging loose today. "I know. It's totally uncool."

"Maybe we could just start over?"

"How?"

"You said we could be friends. Let's really try, okay? I'm stuck on this scene in the book. Maybe you could help me. When are you off today?"

"Three."

"Okay, yeah, let's get together and talk about work. We might as well. I need your help."

Pete seemed to be internally debating but he finally said, "Where should we meet?"

Jack's first instinct was Kingston's place, but the proximity of the large, comfortable bed made him uneasy. "Nina's?"

Pete shook his head. Perhaps he was thinking the cozy Italian place would feel too date-like. Jack mourned the fact that he'd never be taking this gorgeous person on a proper date.

"How about the library? They're open until six on Saturdays."

"The library. Great. Where's that?"

Pete gave him sketchy directions and promised to meet him there a little after three. Jack decided he'd take it, and packed up shortly after, unable to focus while Pete was only a few feet away. It might as well have been a million miles.

A few minutes after Jack decamped the coffee shop, Meadow cornered Pete by the dairy fridge. "What the heck was all that with you and the pretty boy?"

"What are you talking about?"

"Oh please, you guys were giving each other the biggest, saddest, most pathetic cow eyes I've ever seen. You looked like babies who'd lost their wubbies."

"What's a wubbie?" Pete asked quizzically.

"You know, like a security blanket? It's not important. The important thing is why you two went from Prom King and King to looking like you just found out you're actually brothers or something."

Pete couldn't help a snort-laugh. "Okay, it's not that. But we did find out that we actually work together. That we already knew each other professionally by different names."

"So?" Meadow tapped her black-painted nails on the counter impatiently.

Pete grabbed a rag and started wiping down the stainless-steel dairy fridge. "So, whatever might have been brewing between us romantically is off the table now."

"Why?"

"Because it is, okay? I can't date a coworker. It's the worst idea in the world."

"The worst idea in the world is mixing Mentos and soda. What's so bad about dating a coworker?"

"It's messy and dangerous and nothing is worth the complication."

"You sound like someone who got burned real bad," Meadow said, her tone shifting from skeptically abrasive to sympathetic in an instant.

He thought about Kurt, about how he'd trusted him so quickly, so fully, and how he'd abused his trust to a point where Pete lost his job, his apartment, his credibility in some circles, not to mention his credit rating. After Kurt was done with him, he probably couldn't have qualified for another place in the city.

Carol hadn't bothered to run a credit check on him, and he paid her in cash.

"Third degree burns," he muttered.

"But Jack's not like that," Meadow said.

"How do you know?" he asked almost viciously, though he knew intellectually she was probably right. He didn't know Jack very well, but he knew Kingston. He didn't work with flakes or fools. Hell, Pete himself had known Jonathan, if only through email, for a couple of years now. He was, by all indications, a good guy.

But Pete couldn't do it. And it sucked, big time. Because Jack was still Jack, even if he was Jonathan, too. He was sweet and soft and had those clear, imploring eyes, and a mouth that made you want to give up everything you believed in just to get a single taste.

Pete was strong, though. He was a survivor. And when Jack left to go back to the city, he'd still have Rosedale, he'd have the small, stable world he'd built out of literally nothing.

He just wouldn't have Jack.

Chapter 8

The Rosedale Library was not what Jack had been expecting. He loved libraries even more than he loved bookstores, but this one seemed like it could use some TLC, or some tax dollars. It consisted of two musty rooms in a shabby building on a side street off the main drag.

He arrived before Pete and poked around, then met the librarian on duty, a middle-aged woman named Sandra who kind of reminded him of his mama. She told him the story while he put all the cash in his wallet in the donation box. Apparently, the library had once been housed in a beautiful stone building on the other side of town, but it burned in a fire a few years ago and the rebuilding plans had been suspended in a nightmarish snare of insurance claims and counterclaims. In the meantime, the town had given them this space, but they barely had enough room to act as a repository for what books survived the fire, let alone fulfill their mission of programming for the community.

Jack frowned. A town like Rosedale should have a library it could be proud of.

He thanked Sandra and found a spot on a table in the main room and opened his laptop. He hadn't been putting Pete on when he'd said he could use his help with the book. He was stuck, again, and maybe Pete could work his magic and get the words flowing.

Pete walked in closer to three thirty than three, his face tight. He let his phone clatter to the table and pulled out a chair, scraping the feet along the hard linoleum floor with a screech.

"What's wrong?" Jack asked. He'd never seen Pete look this stormy.

"I—nothing," Pete said, scowling at his phone. "Let's just work."

Jack knew Pete wanted to keep his personal life and their professional lives separate, but this seemed excessive. Still, he was trying to respect the boundaries Pete had so firmly established the night before.

"Okay. I'm at around the two-thirds mark. Rupert and Drew have a plan to defeat the new kid who's bullying Drew's friend Corrina, but once that's resolved, I want to advance their arc."

Pete pulled out the little notebook Jack had seen him with before. "Advance how?"

"Well, they've gone from enemies to allies, and they need to finally acknowledge their friendship."

"Okay." Pete started sketching with a mechanical pencil that came out with the notebook. Jack watched his hands as they moved. They were so big, they dwarfed the slim drawing implement and the rectangle of paper, but they moved with grace. He had a steady, sure hand and he made lines on the paper as Jack continued to talk through ideas he'd had.

Pete kept his eyes on the notebook, so Jack felt free to keep his on Pete. As they talked and batted ideas back and forth, the tension seemed to seep out of Pete's shoulders, and he even smiled once or twice. Jack considered it a personal victory when he made Pete laugh, bright and loud in the cramped space.

Eventually, one of the ideas caught hold in Jack's imagination, and he started typing. He was a pretty fast typist, but even he couldn't keep watching Pete and write sentences that made any sense whatsoever, and he reluctantly focused on the screen, writing rough notes at this point, but he had a good sense of where the next few scenes were going to go by the time Pete said, "What do you think of this?"

Pete held up his notebook and Jack stopped typing, looking at the drawing closely.

Drew and Rupert mid-conversation, Rupert's hair messy in a way that made Jack feel seen. He peered at Drew, at the slope of his nose and the slant of his eyes. He glanced up at Pete. "I never realized it until now, but Drew looks a little like you."

Pete snapped the notebook shut. "Really?" He looked down. "I guess I identified with him unconsciously. Sorry."

"Don't apologize, Pete. Your Drew is perfect." *You're perfect*, Jack wanted to say. "And I think we're on the right track. You don't know how much this helps me. Seriously. I was banging my head against the wall this morning."

Pete reopened the notebook, paging through the sketches he'd made during their work session. "I think some of these are usable, but I'll have to recreate them on my tablet at home."

"I'd love to learn more about your process," Jack said. He wanted to know everything about Pete, but he'd settle for keeping it all about work. They did seem to work well together, after all.

"It's not that exciting," Pete said.

"Considering I can't draw to save my life, I'm pretty confident that anything you'd show me would blow my mind." He caught Pete's gaze and held it. While it was gratifying to know they worked well together, he still missed the flirty, enthusiastic Pete. P.J. Blue was so talented, but he had walls up a mile high. "And you never answered my question from yesterday. Why P.J. Blue? And why work at Hot Brew when you're a working artist?"

Pete blew out a breath. Jack was afraid he wasn't going to answer, but then he said, "My real last name is Blekitny. When I got to New York and started submitting to shows and galleries, I got the advice to simplify. Blekitny's Polish for blue. I started selling way more stuff as P.J. Blue than as Peter Jacob Blekitny. Art's a business that cares a lot about what's on the surface."

"Peter Jacob Blekitny," Jack said,

committing the name to memory. He liked it. "P.J. Blue works, but I like Pete. Suits you."

Pete smiled a little at that. "What about you, *Jonathan*?"

Jack ignored the prickle of arousal in his gut at hearing Pete call him by his proper name and answered. "My parents named me after my uncle, so they called me Jack to tell us apart."

Pete wrinkled his brow. "Wait, isn't there a Jonathan Avery in Texas politics?"

"Uh, yeah. That's my uncle." Jack hoped Pete would leave it at that but—

"And isn't he from some big oil family? Are you—are you one of *those* Averys?"

Jack internally sighed. He'd left Texas to avoid being stereotyped as one of "those Averys," political conservatives who had grown their wealth in the generations since a lucky ancestor had struck oil on his otherwise barren Texas ranch.

"In name only," he promised. "My parents are the black sheep of the family." He decided not to mention the trust fund that enabled him to live in Manhattan on an author's income. The Super Rupert books sold well, but he would never have been able to afford his lifestyle in those years after college and before they sold without the dividends from his trust. But he didn't think Pete wanted to hear about that when he worked at a coffee shop to pay the rent.

"Okay," Pete said, though he didn't sound convinced. "You might as well know, I work at Hot Brew because I like it, but also because my ex left me broke and ruined my credit. Right before we met this afternoon, I got a call from a debt collector who claims I owe them because Kurt defaulted on a loan they say I co-signed. Which I never did."

Jack covered up his shock that someone would treat Pete like that with a practical solution. "Sounds like you need a lawyer."

"Yeah, I can pay for one with tips from the lunch rush," Pete said caustically. Then he shoved his hands through his hair. "Look, I'm sorry. My financial problems are not your issue."

Jack wanted to tell Pete it was all going to be okay; he wanted to wave a magic wand and fix it. But he wasn't living in a fairy tale. "I'm sorry. That really sucks. Will you please tell me if there's anything I can do to help? I mean it." He was almost a hundred percent certain that Pete wouldn't ask him for a thing, but he had to make the offer, anyway.

Pete's mouth softened. "Thanks. I'll figure something out."

"Are we still going to meet up for our walk and the farmer's market tomorrow?" Jack said casually, not wanting to get his hopes up.

Pete fiddled with his pencil. "Don't you need to work?"

"I could use a day off," Jack said. It wasn't strictly true—he needed to finish the book; his deadline loomed. But he was determined to soak up as much time with Pete as he'd give him. "And I could use the exercise."

"All right. Meet me at the cemetery at nine."

"Awesome," Jack said, trying not to let his grin get too big. "Doing anything fun tonight?"

Pete laughed humorlessly. "I was going to meet up with some friends to see a movie in Midville." The nearest big town had the closest movie theater. "But being harassed by debt collectors killed my movie mojo."

"You should go," Jack urged. Even if he couldn't be there for Pete the way he wanted to, it would do Pete good to be with friends instead of being alone. "It's Saturday night. Have some fun."

Pete stared at him, studying his face and Jack worried he had the remnants of lunch on his chin.

"You're right. Thanks, Jack. You know, I think this book is going to be really good."

Jack relaxed and told himself to be happy that at least they made good work partners.

"And I know I've been kind of a jerk about

this…situation we're in. I wanted to say I'm sorry."

"It's okay," Jack said. The little he'd learned about Pete's foul ex was giving him a clue as to why Pete was taking it slow.

"And…" Pete took a deep breath, as if he was steeling himself to do something unpleasant. "Drawing for Super Rupert has been the best job I've ever had. But I'm a little sad that you turned out to be…you. Because I think you're amazing. And I wanted you to know that, even if it doesn't change anything."

Goosebumps rose on Jack's skin in the tepid air of the dilapidated library. Pete thought he was amazing. He let the knowledge buoy him as he and Pete parted ways, reaffirming their plans for a Sunday morning walk and farmer's market excursion. Even if they were getting together as friends, as co-workers, it was enough. For now.

Chapter 9

Jack was late.

Pete shifted from foot to foot nervously. Was he being stood up? He couldn't be stood up because this wasn't a date. This was two friends-slash-co-workers meeting up for a morning walk and a quick, casual farmer's market hang.

If his hands hadn't been busy holding two cups of coffee, he would have slapped himself on the forehead. He was skating on thin ice—it wasn't like two gay guys couldn't go to a farmer's market together without it being romantic. But he'd told Jack he thought he was amazing. And when he finally spotted Jack trudging through the cemetery a minute later, the morning sun glinting off his messy hair, his shoulders limned in light and his pretty eyes squinting sleepily, Pete had to admit—to himself if to no one else—that not only was Jack amazing, Pete had it bad.

"Sorry, I overslept." Jack's voice was rough, as if he'd just rolled out of bed.

Pete wished he could have been there when Jack woke up, rubbing the sleep from his eyes, all warm and rumpled. When he'd been the one crashing at Kingston's, he'd slept in the bed Jack had most likely slept in last night. He could picture it, the big, comfy king, Jack laid out against the sheets—

Shit. Pete blinked, handed Jack the coffee he'd brought him from Hot Brew.

"Here," he said shortly, to stop himself from further useless thoughts. He'd had trouble sleeping, gotten up early and put in a workout at the community center, then stopped by Hot

Brew for breakfast and caffeine. He'd figured he might as well bring Jack a cup while he was at it. Now he wished he'd brought Jack a bear claw, too. He probably hadn't eaten yet.

"You're a lifesaver," Jack said, taking the cup gratefully. "Wanna walk?"

They went down the familiar path, not talking. It wasn't awkward. Jack was clearly still waking up, and Pete was trying to get his libido under control. He didn't know where all of this was coming from—okay, that wasn't strictly true. He hadn't had sex in a long time and Jack was hot enough to turn on a dead person.

But he didn't want to want Jack.

They were still finding their footing after finding out their other identities. And Pete had a feeling there was a lot more to learn about Jack. Just yesterday, he'd discovered that Jack was from a big, wealthy, politically connected family. Pete's parents were humble public school teachers. Jack clearly had means—even his rental car was nice. Pete was still trying to figure out how to prove to the bank that Kurt had forged his signature on the papers for the loan he'd apparently defaulted on.

He sighed. He'd work something out. It had taken him too long to figure out that Kurt was using him, but he was doing okay now. He had a job, a place to live, friends. Jack was right—going to the movies to see a terrible comedy had been the perfect thing to do to get his mind off his troubles. He glanced sideways as they reached the part of the trail that started to loop back to the cemetery. Jack looked more awake. He looked beautiful, really, in the dappled morning sunlight.

Pete realized with a blinding, terrible certainty that he wanted to kiss his friend. He wanted to step in, cradle Jack's model-perfect jawline and kiss him, consequences be damned. Jack was so good, and Pete was tired of having to be careful. He was almost certain that Jack wouldn't hurt him—not on purpose, anyway. He took a half step in Jack's direction, when a fluffy medium-sized dog bounded around the curve in the trail ahead of them.

The dog made a beeline for Jack, whose face lit up in delight. He opened his palm for the dog to sniff, then started rubbing behind its ears.

A man's voice called out, "Daisy, be good," before he came into sight on the path.

"Heya, Daisy. You're a sweetheart," Jack cooed, and Pete's heart took a dive off a very tall cliff. He'd thought Jack couldn't get any more perfect and there he went, going all doe-eyed over a dog.

Motherfucker didn't play fair.

Daisy's owner tried to get her to heel, but she was more interested in being loved on by Jack. Pete didn't blame her. The guy wasn't bad to look at—dark brown skin and eyes, generous mouth and quick smile—but when Jack was rubbing behind your ears, you stayed put.

"She likes you, obviously," he said to Jack, bending over to clip Daisy's lead to her collar. "Sorry about that."

"No worries," Jack said, smiling at the guy. "She looks like a dog I had when I was a kid."

"I get that a lot. She's got that generic every-dog look, don't you, baby?" he said, looking fondly at the dog. His gaze was just as warm when he looked at Jack.

Pete's jaw tightened.

"I'm Sergio," he said, offering a hand to Jack, who shook it easily.

"Jack," he said. "This is Pete."

"Hi," Sergio said, giving Pete a chin lift, then immediately looking back at Jack. Because of course. Jack was a planet with a gravitational field all his own. Pete was barely hovering in his orbit. "You local? I just got a weekend place nearby, and I'd love a local's perspective."

"Pete's the Rosedale evangelist," Jack said with a laugh. "I'm just a temporary city transplant."

"Oh yeah? Where in the city?" Sergio asked.

"Harlem," Jack said. "Morningside Heights."

"No way. I'm in Spanish Harlem." Sergio sounded thrilled about their neighborhood proximity. The two of them started chatting about their favorite spots in their corner of Manhattan while Pete took his turn petting Daisy's head. She was a sweetie, and Pete loved dogs. No reason to ignore her just because her owner was blatantly flirting with the guy Pete had inappropriate, inconvenient feelings for.

Jack laughed at something Sergio said, and Pete narrowed his eyes. Sergio flirting with Jack was one thing, but was Jack flirting *back*?

Well, why shouldn't he? Pete didn't have any claim on him. In fact, he'd told him they couldn't be in a romantic relationship. Of course he was free to flirt with whatever cute dog owner came along.

Pete suddenly felt a little sick. He broke into the conversation. "If you want to get to know Rosedale, you can start at the farmer's market. It's on until one. Jack and I were on our way there."

Sergio looked slightly surprised at Pete's contribution, as if he'd already forgotten about him. "Farmer's market. Thanks for the tip." He pulled out his phone. "Can't make it there today, unfortunately. Jack, let me get your digits and I'll text you the name of that restaurant."

Pete clamped his lips shut and listened to Jack reel off his number. Jack gave Daisy one more scrub on the head and then she and Sergio took off down the path the way he and Jack had come.

Jack started walking forward to complete the loop. "Nice guy," he said.

"Real smooth," Pete said, internally wincing at how bitter he sounded.

Jack gave him a look. "What's up with you?"

"Sorry, it's just that he got your 'digits' really fast."

Jack stopped on the trail. "You jealous?"

"No," Pete lied. "I just worry about you. People are weird."

"I can take care of myself," Jack said mildly. "But your concern is noted."

They walked back to the trailhead in silence. When they got there, Pete was relieved that Sergio and Daisy were nowhere to be seen.

"You must be starving," he said. "There's a food truck that makes amazing breakfast sandwiches at the market."

"I'm getting two," Jack said, patting his belly. "Let's go in my car. It's already starting to heat up."

It was one of those crystal clear, unusually dry July days. The air conditioning in Jack's rental car was a welcome reprieve, but it was another reminder that Jack was way out of Pete's league.

"So one of the reasons I overslept was I was up late talking to my brother," Jack said, as he looked for a parking place.

"There's one." Pete pointed, and Jack slid

the car into the space. "I didn't know you had a brother."

"Christopher. He's a lawyer. Corporate law, but he told me he could give me the name of someone who might be able to help with that loan thing you were telling me about."

Pete froze. He didn't know how to feel. Jack was being Jack, wanting to help, but it just made Pete feel worse that Jack thought he needed his help at all. It was probably some fucked up toxic masculinity thing, but Pete didn't want to be a damsel that Jack had to save.

"And I know you didn't ask me to do that, and maybe you don't want my help, but I just had to. What your ex did to you—is still doing to you—that's not right. And if I can help, I want to. I like to help my friends," Jack said firmly.

Pete let out a hot breath. He got out of the car, suddenly feeling stifled in the small space. A delicious aroma emanated from the food trucks, and someone was strumming on a guitar nearby. Friends. Right. He'd told Jack they could be friends and Jack was taking him at his word.

He closed his eyes against the bright summer sun. He wished he'd brought sunglasses. He huffed out an unhappy laugh. If he mentioned that, Jack would probably produce an extra pair from someplace, or dash into a store to buy him some. Pete balled his hands into fists, paradoxically trying to relax. Jack was just being Jack. And Pete was slowly and surely falling for him.

How had things gotten so twisted in so short a time? From strangers to almost-dates, to finding out they already knew each other, to working together, to friends, and now to this horrible in-between where Pete wanted to kiss Jack and work alongside him and take him to bed and let him solve all his problems and introduce him to his parents someday.

It had all spun out of Pete's control, and he'd only just gotten control back after Kurt.

He opened his eyes when he heard Jack shut the driver's door and walk over.

"Are you okay? Did I mess up? You don't have to talk to the lawyer if you don't want to, but they'd give you some advice for free as a favor to Christopher."

"You didn't mess up. And that's so nice of your brother—of you. You didn't have to. You're a good person, Jack."

Jack shrugged, clearly uncomfortable. "I'm just—I just want to help," he said again, in a small voice.

"I know. Thank you."

"So you'll talk to them?" Jack said hopefully.

"Yeah. Sure. I'll talk to them." Pete said, knowing it would be foolish to let his pride stop him from accepting Jack's offer.

"Great. I'm sure there's something they can do," Jack said, sounding relieved as if he was the one who was in trouble and might have a way out. "Now, how about those breakfast sandwiches?"

Pete wasn't hungry, but he followed Jack to the food truck and ordered one anyway. He had a feeling Jack would worry if he didn't eat.

"What about you? Do you have any brothers or sisters?" Jack asked while they waited for their meal.

"I have a little sister," Pete said. "She's in college. Austin. Probably going to be a teacher like my parents."

"Cool. I wish I had the patience to be a teacher. You teach, too, don't you? At the Art Center?"

"That's different. It's mostly adults. Retirees and stay at home parents."

"So? Teaching is teaching."

Pete had never thought of it that way. "I guess. Is Christopher your only sibling?"

"I've got a little sister, too, about your age. She's in med school."

"Wow, lawyer, doctor, and...children's book author?" Pete lifted his eyebrows.

"Yeah." Jack laughed. "I'm lucky my parents think having a writer for a son is actually more interesting than the lawyer and the doctor."

"They sound cool."

"They're a little young to be hippies, but if they'd been old enough, they would have been very Summer of Love types," he said. "They'll probably adore you. Dad's always fancied himself an artist. He makes sculptures out of junk. And Mama has always worked for nonprofits. Her latest one brings arts education to underfunded schools."

Their numbers were called at the window of the food truck. They took their steaming hot sandwiches to a bench in the shade.

"They're still in Texas?" Pete asked.

"Yeah, but they come to visit me at least once a year. They love New York."

"My parents never come to the city," Pete said. "Way too exciting for them."

They ate and talked, and Pete forgot for a little while all the reasons he and Jack didn't make sense, because he was enjoying simply getting to know him better. Eventually, they got up and made their way down the row of vendors. Jack grabbed some jars of jam and local honey he said would make good gifts, and Pete got some bread he told Carol he'd pick up for her.

"We should go out tonight," Jack declared, once they'd seen everything the Rosedale farmer's market had to offer. "What's your poison?"

"What do you mean?" Pete said. The warm summer air was making him pleasantly drowsy.

"I'm a beer man, usually," Jack said. "But sometimes I like to go wild. Then I go for margaritas."

Pete laughed. "Would not have pegged you for a margarita guy."

"So what about you?" Jack pressed.

Pete had trained himself to like cheap beer and well vodka, but when things had been going better for him, after Super Rupert took off and he'd had that gallery show, he'd enjoyed splurging on good bourbon. "Um, I like a whiskey sour," he said, not sure why he was suddenly feeling bashful about his drinking preferences. It's not like Jack was going to judge him.

"Classy," was all Jack said. "So, does that Irish pub do a good whiskey sour?" He pointed to the bar down the street that Pete had been to a few times with Meadow and Che.

"It isn't bad," he said, still not quite sure where Jack was going with this.

"I've got some things to take care of this afternoon. Meet me there around eight?"

Pete mentally reviewed his social calendar; his evening plans consisted of laundry and leftovers. Going drinking at a bar with Jack? How bad of an idea could it be?

Chapter 10

Jack pulled into the parking lot of the supermarket but didn't get out of the car. He had mixed feelings about finally doing the shopping he'd been meaning to do since his arrival in Rosedale. On the one hand, it would be nice to be less dependent on the restaurants in town. On the other hand, he might not be there that long and he didn't want to be wasteful.

He'd been up last night late talking to Christopher about a variety of things, as well as reviewing his progress on the book. With the notes he and Pete made at the library, he could see the end in sight. His deadline was less than two weeks away now, and he probably only needed a handful of days to complete the draft and go through it closely enough to be ready for the editor.

Once he turned in the draft there would be no reason to stick around Rosedale. He'd go back to New York, retrieve his succulent plant from his neighbor, air out his apartment. He'd take care of things he'd let pile up while he was on his strange work retreat and wait for the notes to come back on the Super Rupert book, after which he'd do a round of revisions. When the story was locked, Pete would be sent the manuscript with the list of suggested illustrations. He'd be busy working on those while Jack would turn his attention to the layers of editorial that remained, working out his schedule for promotion and marketing of the book. Due to his procrastination, they'd be busy all fall in order to get the book ready for a holiday release.

There would be no reason to stick around Rosedale, except that's where Pete was.

Jack had only known him for a few days, truly known him, that is, but he could admit he'd gotten attached in that short time. It wasn't as if they'd never see each other again once Jack returned to the city. Rosedale was two hours away by car, a little longer by train. And maybe distance from Jack was what Pete needed. Maybe Jack needed it, too.

Things had gotten intense quickly. It wasn't like Jack to feel as if he couldn't walk away from a guy. He'd been in a couple of longer-term relationships, but they always seemed to run their course. The reasons he got together with someone—mutual attraction, mutual friends—weren't enough to keep them going for the long haul.

At his core, he wanted what his parents had —a partnership. Not always easy, but with a strong foundation that was sturdy enough to withstand the rocky times. He couldn't know that Pete was that person—it was too soon to tell, by all reasonable measures.

But Jack had never felt this mixture of fondness, protectiveness, and lust before. He'd never been in so much awe of someone and still wanted to tuck them to his side and walk through life with them. He felt like in Pete he had found someone who would be a true partner, someone who would support him and challenge him and someone he wanted to take care of. Someone he'd let take care of him.

It should have been too soon, but it wasn't. Jack knew what he wanted.

However, clearly Pete wasn't on the same page. Jack had never thought of himself as a patient man, but he knew the stakes were high enough with Pete that he'd wait as long as he had to.

But he wasn't above greasing the wheels a little. Which was where the invitation to the bar came in. In vino veritas and all that.

He sighed. It was probably a stupid plan.

He'd most likely end the night tipsy and wanting Pete more than ever, while he stayed depressingly out of reach. And yet...there was something there— Jack was sure of it. He'd thought on the trail that morning that Pete might kiss him. And then they'd met Daisy and Sergio and while Jack was always happy to meet a cool dog and their cool owner, the glint of jealousy in Pete's eyes and the set of his jaw had made Jack happier than Daisy's affectionate slobbering. He'd been worried he'd gone too far when he told Pete about Christopher's offer to help, but Pete had accepted relatively graciously, and Jack was relieved that someone with more expertise than he would be able to give Pete a hand. He knew there was more to the story with Pete's ex, and since every piece he learned was worse than the one before, he was almost afraid to ask.

He grabbed the pile of reusable bags he'd found in Kingston's hall closet. He might as well buy some food. He might not be in Rosedale long enough to use it up, but then again, he'd been surprised more than once this week.

Before he could get out, his phone rang. Kingston's name flashed on the screen. He hit a button and his agent's voice flooded the car's cabin.

"Jack, my friend, tell me everything. What did I miss?"

"Where the hell have you been?" Jack had texted Kingston half a dozen times since the night of the Art Center dinner where he'd discovered that Pete and P.J. Blue were one and the same. Kingston had only responded to one of the messages, saying he would call when he had a minute.

"'My mom had a slight heart episode, but she came home from the hospital yesterday, so things are good." Kingston sounded matter of fact but also a little tired now that Jack was paying attention.

"Jesus, I'm so sorry." Jack immediately felt terrible. His agent was such a force of nature that he sometimes forgot he had a life outside of the book world.

"It was scary for a minute but she's going to be fine. My sister flew in from Chicago to help so I'm finally going through the pile up on my desk. Your texts alluded to drama. Only you could find drama in Rosedale, Connecticut, Avery."

"Why didn't you tell me P.J. Blue lived here?" Jack said, figuring neither of them wanted to waste time beating around the bush.

There was a beat of silence. "Well now, that's a good question. I take it you ran into your illustrious illustrator?"

"You could say that," Jack said mildly. "Only when we met, he was using his real name, and since he only knew me as Jonathan, not Jack, it took us a little while to figure out we already knew each other."

Kingston laughed. "Seriously? You guys met and then figured out your alter egos? Very Clark Kent of you."

"It was fine, at first, because you know I

love the art for Super Rupert, and Pete is cool, so it was kind of awesome to find out they're the same person. But." Jack hoped his tone would convey all the complexity of their relationship in that single conjunction. "It would have been nice to have a heads up is all."

"Look, I've known Pete longer than I've known you, and while you are both a client and a friend, he was going through a rough time and it honestly didn't occur to me when I offered you my place that you might end up meeting, or that it would cause any issues between you. I'm surprised you never met before. He lived in the city until recently."

Jack knew it was irrational to expect two random people to meet in a city of millions, but he was a little surprised, too. The New York City gay community wasn't tiny, but sometimes Manhattan felt more like a small town than a big city. Ironically, he'd had to come to an actual small town to meet the man of his dreams.

Oh god, he was so fucked. "Kingston, I'm in trouble."

"You are not missing that deadline, Jack," Kingston said fiercely. "Not if I have to physically push your fingers down on the keyboard myself."

"No, it's not that. The book's going to be done. Thanks to Pete. He got me moving on the story again." He swallowed and continued softly. "He's wonderful."

"Oh. I see." Kingston sighed. "Again, I've known Pete a long time. He's a good guy. And now that I'm thinking about it, I can see it. You two. Two gorgeous tall drinks of water. If you could have babies, they'd be stunning. But he went through some shit. You need to be careful."

"I know. Don't worry. We're both putting the project first. Super Rupert is going to be done on time. It might even be the best one in the series so far."

"As your agent, I'm thrilled. But that's not

what I meant. I don't want to see either of you get hurt."

"Thanks." Jack rubbed his eyes tiredly. "Well, we're doing the friends thing. The co-worker thing. That's all Pete wants, anyway."

"He said that?"

The vision of Pete glancing at his mouth, taking a step forward, before Daisy came bounding up that morning swam in front of Jack. He pushed it away. "Yeah."

"It'll be okay. You're both due for a win. Get Super Rupert turned in and we'll celebrate."

"I'm on it. Now, stop worrying about my pathetic ass and focus on your family. I hope your mom feels better soon." He made a mental note to send flowers.

"Thanks. I will. But I'm here if you need me. Pete, too."

They hung up and Jack went to get a shopping cart. He wasn't giving up on Rosedale, or on Pete, anytime soon.

Chapter 11

Pete hesitated outside the door to the pub. He'd spent the afternoon doing chores and laundry and after eating a dinner of leftovers he'd put on a denim button-down instead of his usual black one, feeling mildly foolish. This wasn't a date, so it didn't matter how he looked.

Then again, how many not-a-dates did he and Jack have to go on before Pete would be able to admit that he wanted Jack as a friend and co-worker, and also wanted him, period? He wanted Jack against a wall or underneath him, in the backseat of his rental car or in Kingston's guest bed. Hell, he'd settle for holding hands at this point.

He'd been denying himself and he was tired of it, tired of himself, tired of giving control of his life over to the phantom of Kurt's betrayals.

Once he walked through that door, he had to be honest. He had to tell Jack how he felt. And maybe that meant he'd get hurt, sooner or later, but moving forward was better than this limbo he'd placed them in, where they were so careful around each other, as if each had his hands covered in bubble wrap lest they reach out and break something unintentionally.

Well, Pete was tearing off the bubble wrap, and while he was at it, he might as well yank off the layer of it that had encased his heart for too long.

He pushed his way inside, spotted Jack immediately. He was in a small booth, looking at the one-page menu. His crisp white button down glowed in the dim light of the bar. His hair was slightly less messy than usual, and Pete's breath quickened when Jack looked up, saw him, and smiled.

To be the person who Jack smiled at like that—Pete didn't know what he'd done to deserve that, but he was determined not to let his chance slip away.

He walked up to the booth, channeling confidence that had come so easily before Kurt. "You clean up nice, Mr. Avery."

Jack's smile grew into a grin. "You're looking good, too, Mr. Blekitny."

Pete bit down on the inside of his cheek to keep from smiling too hard. Things were already moving, and they hadn't even had anything to drink yet.

He glanced at the bar, wondering if he should get them a round, but then a girl in a T-shirt with the bar's logo emblazoned on it came up and asked what they wanted to drink.

"Whiskey sour?" Jack asked Pete.

He slid into the booth across from Jack. "Sure. Margarita?"

Jack laughed. "Why not? Give my friend the best bourbon you've got for that whiskey sour, please. I'll take that fancy tequila I see on the shelf there. Rocks and salt, please."

The girl looked between the two of them, smiled a little, and told them she'd be back.

"This round's on me, by the way," Jack said. "I hope you had a good rest of your Sunday."

"It wasn't bad. What did you do?"

"A little shopping. And I talked to our mutual friend, the one and only Kingston James."

"How's he doing?"

"His mom was in the hospital, actually, but he said she's going to be fine."

"Oh shit, sorry to hear that." Pete hadn't spoken to Kingston in a while, but he was good people. "Does he need anything?"

"He says he's okay. He was happy when I told him the book would be turned in on time."

That was better news. "You're sure?"

"Yesterday really helped. I think I only need a few more days to finish writing the thing."

Jack fiddled with the menu. "Actually, I was hoping you'd read it and give me your notes before I send it to the editor."

Pete squinted. He'd never seen an early draft of a Super Rupert book before. "That's not usually part of the deal, is it?"

"The editor doesn't need to know. I'd really like to hear what you think."

He hesitated. The reminder that he and Jack had to work together was a spray of cold water on his plan. But maybe it was time for him to be brave. "Of course I'd like to read it," he said slowly. "I'd be honored, Jack."

Jack looked relieved. "Great. Thanks. I really couldn't have gotten this far with the series without your help."

"It's been a fantastic gig," Pete said, honestly. He fiddled with the coaster on the table in front of him. "I know I've been weird about us working together."

"It's okay," Jack said quickly. "I don't regret anything."

"That's because you're incredibly nice,"

Pete said, summoning up all his courage. "But I owe you more of an explanation."

"You don't owe me anything," Jack said.

The server returned with their drinks. Jack thanked her and opened a tab. "You want something to eat?" he asked Pete.

"Maybe later."

She left and Jack raised his glass. "What should we drink to?"

"Um...Super Rupert?" Pete suggested.

"To Super Rupert," Jack repeated.

Pete tapped his glass against Jack's with a satisfying clink.

The first taste went down easy, the second even easier. Jack seemed to enjoy the flavor of his margarita just as much. He took another sip and Pete had to tear his eyes away from the way Jack's lips glistened after his pink tongue flicked out to lick away the salt.

"Anyway, I need to tell you a couple of things, just so you get where I'm coming from."

"All right," Jack said, easy and open and so

pretty Pete really wanted to skip to the part where they'd figured everything out and were making out already. But first things first.

"You know I had a bad breakup, and that money was involved. I'm not going to go into a blow by blow of all the sordid details, but what you should probably know was that Kurt and I worked together." He looked carefully at Jack, but aside from a slight muscle twitch in his jaw, he didn't move.

"We met at a gallery show. This was over two years ago now, after I'd done the first Super Rupert book but before it started selling. He was an art agent who had just moved to New York from L.A., and I was twenty-six and sick of retail jobs and looking for a way into the art world. He was charming, we hit it off, and he took me on as a client. He booked my first group show and got me a couple of commissions. I thought things were going great. Then he asked me out." He took a deep breath. This was the hard part. "I was young and dumb, and I thought, wow, this is the best of all worlds. He's older, attractive, he believes in my work. I fell in love."

Pete paused to take a sip of his drink, and Jack did the same. Had he imagined Jack's mouth tightening when he said he fell in love? He didn't want to hurt Jack, but he needed him to know everything.

"But after a few months, the red flags started popping up. He told me I sold a painting for a thousand dollars, and by accident I saw the bill of sale. He'd charged the buyer four times that much and pocketed the three grand, plus the commission on the thousand he told me about. When I confronted him, he totally gaslighted me, and since he said he was about to book me a solo show, I decided to overlook it. I just kept ignoring all the bad shit because he said all the right things, made me believe all the success I'd had since we met was because of him and not me busting my ass to both produce and do the New York art scene rounds."

He remembered how hard he'd worked

during that period. He had left his retail job but was working part time at the coffee bar in a museum, then spending his afternoons and evenings in the small studio space he rented, going out late with Kurt to parties and gallery openings. He'd exhausted himself and couldn't figure out why he didn't have more to show for it. He knew he was selling pieces, plus the royalty checks from Super Rupert started to come in, but he never seemed to have much left over after Kurt took his cut.

"At one point, he said he needed a loan to invest in a gallery so the owners would give me a show. I believed him, and that's where most of my royalties from the first couple of books went. Anyway, long story short, I ignored all the signs because I was afraid if I cut ties with him, he'd badmouth me to the gallery owners. Plus, I thought I loved him."

Jack winced, turning his glass around in his hands, but he said nothing.

"Turns out, I loved the idea of someone who understood me and my work, who supported my dreams of being a working artist. What I couldn't ignore was catching him with his hands down the pants of a friend of mine at a party. In the coat check. How cliché can you get?"

"Jesus. I'm so sorry, Pete." Jack's voice was low and sincere.

"Once I ended our relationship, I found out he'd had to leave L.A. because he'd embezzled funds from a client out there. I kissed the money I'd lent him goodbye, then found out he'd also drained my savings account, taken out a line of credit in my name, maxed it out, and hadn't paid a dime on it. So my credit was wrecked, and I got fired from the coffee bar because I was missing so much work trying to clean up the mess he'd left me with. I couldn't make my rent. It was, to put it mildly, a disaster. That's when I pulled up stakes. I thought if I could get out of the city for a while, I could get my head on straight. But the longer I stay away, the harder it feels like it's going to be to go back. My reputation might never recover. I'll be washed up at twenty-eight. Well, twenty-nine."

Jack cocked his head. "Which is it?"

"I'll be twenty-nine tomorrow," Pete said, a little shyly. He hadn't told any of his friends from Hot Brew or the Art Center about his birthday.

"Tomorrow's your birthday?" Jack grinned. "That's it—next round's on me, too."

Pete allowed him to signal to the server for another round. Somehow, he'd sucked his whiskey sour down to the ice, but he wasn't feeling it yet.

"So that's my tale of woe," he said, leaning back from the table, wondering if he felt better or worse after spilling his guts.

"I'm really glad you told me," Jack said. "And it sounds like this Kurt jerk off should be in prison. Embezzlement for starters. He outright stole from you, Pete."

"I don't know. I kind of don't want to expend any more energy on him than I already have."

"I get that, but he shouldn't get away with that." Jack frowned at his drink. "And I'm sorry he broke your heart."

Pete widened his eyes. "Oh no. He broke my will, maybe. Temporarily. But I'm getting it back. Rosedale has been very therapeutic in that way. But he didn't break my heart. I didn't really love him. I don't know that I've ever been with someone who could break my heart."

Jack lifted his gaze, and they locked stares for a long moment. Pete felt like Jack could read it in his eyes—the truth of that statement. And also the lie. Because Pete had a feeling that if he and Jack actually went for it, if they did this, for real, then it would be all too easy to have his heart broken, because Jack would command more of it than anyone ever had before.

Slowly, Jack licked his lips. Pete imagined they'd taste salty and sour from the margarita.

He barely noticed when the server brought them their second round. He took a sightless swallow, unable to stop looking at Jack, preferring to drink him in, all the beautiful parts of him. The best part was knowing that Jack was just as beautiful inside as he was outside.

"I can't believe your birthday is tomorrow," Jack said, breaking the not-uncomfortable silence.

"Yeah. I sort of forgot with all the excitement this week," Pete said, smiling. What a week it had been.

"Are you doing anything to celebrate? Getting together with friends?"

Pete laughed. "I'm here with you."

"True." Jack looked pleased. He went to take a sip of his fresh drink, and impulsively, Pete put a hand on his wrist to stop him.

"Wait. Um." He took a breath to steady himself and let go when Jack's gaze dropped to where his hand still rested on his warm skin. "Sorry. It's just—I don't want our first kiss to be when we're drunk."

Chapter 12

Jack wasn't sure he'd heard right. Their first kiss? Was that what this had all been about—Pete telling him the full, horrible story of his ex? The fact that he'd dressed in something besides black? Pete had been working up to a kiss?

He pushed his glass away decisively. "I'm not drunk."

"Me either," Pete said, then he looked down as if he was embarrassed to have said anything. Jack thought he was adorable.

But he was also worried that Pete was going to do something he'd later regret. Now he knew the extent to which Kurt had screwed Pete over, it made him even more determined to be someone who put Pete first, always.

"Are you sure that's what you want?" He had to be certain.

Pete raised his head. His beautiful eyes sparkled in the light from the intimate little wall lamp at the end of the booth. "I wanted to kiss you the first time I laid eyes on you."

Wow. Jack swallowed, suddenly nervous. Pete wasn't fucking around. This was real. He was acutely aware this might be the last first kiss he'd ever have. His palms suddenly went sweaty and he strongly wanted another taste of his margarita.

But Pete wanted them sober.

Instead of saying anything, he got up, pivoted around the end of the table, and sat down next to Pete on his side of the booth. Pete didn't have time to move; it was a tight fit. Jack could feel him, warm and solid against the length of his side. He took one of Pete's hands in both of his, lowering them below the table. Nobody in the barely half-full bar was paying them any attention, but he wanted this moment to be for them alone.

"I just want you to know," he said, almost conversationally, even though this felt like the most important conversation he'd ever had, "that I really like you, Pete. I think you're so talented, and brave, and hardworking, and clever, and kind. And I promise I'm not going to do anything to make you regret kissing me."

Pete looked down at their joined hands. He let out a shaky breath, then he looked right at Jack.

"I believe you."

That simple expression of faith made Jack happier than having written a dozen bestsellers. Pete should be able to believe in people, to believe in himself. If Jack had anything to do with getting him to believe, he was happy.

"So we're doing this?"

"Define 'this,'" Pete said with a quirk of his sexy mouth.

"God, this is whatever you want, Pete. Whatever you'll let me have. Because I want—" He stopped, licked his lips. Pete seemed to like it when he did that. "I want quite a lot. As much as you'll let me have."

Pete seemed to give the parameters of what they were about to embark on serious thought. "Let's take it slow, okay? I'd say quite a lot is on the table, but not all at once. If that makes sense?"

"Yes, sure. Sounds great." Jack would have agreed to almost anything at that point. Pete's hand felt so warm and good in his. He could only imagine how the rest of him would feel. If he had to find out slowly, so be it.

"But I was serious about the kissing thing. I think if I can't kiss you soon, I might combust."

Jack let his gaze drop to Pete's mouth. "Well, we can't have that. Here?"

Pete looked around. He bit his lip.

"You can come back to my place. I mean, Kingston's," Jack offered.

"Tempting, but if there's a bed handy, I'm afraid my self control is going to be history."

He chuckled at Pete's honesty. "We could go for a walk."

"How about your car?" Pete said.

"My car?" He hadn't been expecting that.

"Privacy," Pete explained. "And it's a very nice car."

"All right." Jack peeled himself away from Pete to close out his tab, then returned to retrieve him, slipping their hands together once more. They left their barely touched drinks on the table. It was dark outside and cooling off. Jack didn't let go of Pete's hand and Pete didn't pull away. The car was parked under a streetlight that let in a flood of yellow light. "Why don't we go somewhere more private?"

Pete's laugh was almost a giggle. "You wanna take me to Lover's Lane."

"Is there one?" Jack asked hopefully.

Pete's giggle turned into a snort. "I actually have no idea. Probably. But I know somewhere we can go."

Jack reluctantly let go of Pete long enough for them to get in the sedan. He felt the energy between them build with each turn of the wheel as Pete directed him up Rosedale Hill. It was delicious torture having Pete inches away and having to wait. He realized where they were going once he saw the Arts Center sign lit up by his headlights. They pulled into the dark, empty parking lot in front of the building. Jack shut off the engine and cut the lights.

"Dark," he said.

"Yeah." Pete's voice was low and suggestive.

Jack turned and there Pete was, his big, artist's hands cupping Jack's face gently. There wasn't much room to maneuver in the cabin with the center console between them, but maybe that was good because Jack wanted to throw himself at Pete and he physically couldn't.

Carefully, he reached up to touch Pete's shoulders, almost yanking his fingers back when he felt how hot Pete was—he was like a furnace, a really built furnace. He grabbed on just as Pete nudged his nose with his pretty sloped one. Jack tilted his head obediently and was rewarded with Pete's mouth on his. Finally.

He sighed into the kiss. Pete tasted smokey and sweet. Jack had never had a first kiss like this. His earliest first kisses were fumbling and overlaid with embarrassment. In college they were usually drunken and sloppy. Once he started dating properly, they were polite tests of compatibility. And in the last couple of years, they'd gotten fewer and farther between.

But kissing Pete for the first time—it was both the beginning of something and the end of something. The end of old Jack, the closing moment of his life as a person who hadn't yet found The One. No matter what happened between them in the future, Jack himself was changed. He was now someone who had tasted true love, to use a completely hackneyed phrase.

His editor would have inserted an eye roll emoji in the comments if he'd tried to use it in a book. But he didn't care. He would never be the same.

Pete kissed with his whole body, his hands never leaving Jack's skin, his mouth moving expertly, his long, strong body leaning into it, but after a minute Pete pulled away. Jack chased Pete's mouth with his, having not gotten his fill. He had a feeling he never would.

From what he could see of Pete's expression in the semi dark, he looked stunned.

All Jack could think to say was— "Pete."

Pete closed his eyes. "Jack."

"I—that was—was that okay?" Just because that had been life-changing for him didn't mean Pete felt the same way.

Pete's eyes opened. "Was it okay? Was it *okay*? I want to lay you down and spread you out and kiss every inch of you. Jesus. Was it okay," he said, trying to scoff but Jack could hear the wavering underneath.

Jack felt hot all over at the idea of every inch of him being kissed by Pete. "I want that, too."

"Fuck. Whose idea was it to do this in the car? We need a bed," Pete grumbled. "Oh right, it was me."

Jack laughed. "There will be plenty of time for a bed."

Pete half-smiled. "Yeah? What about when the book's done? Aren't you going back to the city?"

He didn't know what to say. This night had blown through all his expectations, and he was grasping for clarity about what his next move should be.

"A lot of people come up here on the weekends," he said tentatively.

"Weekends. Right." Pete shifted back, putting some space between them.

"But I'm not going anywhere. I need to finish the book."

"You know when you turn that book in,

that's when my job really starts, right?" Pete said. "I'm going to be really busy."

He felt a stab of guilt. "I know. It's all my fault for being a lazy ass who couldn't get the book done on time."

"That's not what I'm saying. It's just—you'll go home and I'll be working and…and…" Pete trailed off bleakly.

"Hey, let's not borrow trouble, okay? We can figure it out." Jack would do long distance; he'd do whatever it took to keep Pete in his life.

"Suddenly going slow doesn't seem like such a good idea. It feels like we're running out of time already."

Jack put a hand on Pete's knee, squeezed. "I'm not going anywhere. As much as I want to take you to the nearest available horizontal surface and let you have your way with me, we can wait. Because we do have time. Time to do it right, Pete. I'm not taking this lightly."

"No. I know you aren't. You're—" Pete blew out a loud breath. "You're a little too good to be true, Jack. I'm not afraid you're going to screw me over. I'm afraid I'm going to fuck this up because I let things get so out of hand with Kurt. Why would you want to be with someone who's still getting out of a mess?"

"You've got to stop blaming yourself, Pete. He's the one who took advantage of you. Who stole from you. Who cheated on you. The only thing you did was pick the wrong guy. I know how easy that can be."

"I just can't help thinking if I'd been smarter, or tougher, he wouldn't have been able to do those things to me," Pete said softly.

Jack finally understood that Pete hadn't only been screwed over—he thought he'd brought it on himself. "Look at me, Pete."

Their gazes met, Pete's face pinched and small.

"Listen to me, sweetheart. You didn't deserve what he did to you. You don't deserve to keep suffering because of him. No one deserves to have their life messed up like that, by someone they thought they could trust. Someone they tried to love. It's not your fault, Pete."

Pete moved forward and for a second Jack thought he was going to be kissed again, but instead Pete dropped his head to Jack's shoulder. He wasn't crying, exactly, but his breath was fast, and his arms circled Jack's waist, holding on. Jack hugged him back, this tall, strong man folding himself up to be held. He felt like the most privileged guy on Earth that Pete would pick him, would let him comfort him like this.

"It's okay," Jack said, murmuring more nothings into Pete's soft hair. He held him for a long time, until his back started to twinge from the awkward angle he was sitting at. Pete couldn't have been comfortable, either, contorted as he was with the center console between them. Slowly, he eased his arms and Pete pulled back. He was the most beautiful person Jack had ever seen.

The urge to tell him just how deep his

feelings ran rose from Jack's gut, but he knew that moving too fast would only end up setting them back. Instead he asked, "Are you working tomorrow?"

"Um, no—Meadow told me to take my birthday off."

"Good. Let me take you somewhere to celebrate."

"What about the book?"

"I can afford to take one more day," Jack said with more confidence than he felt. "It's your birthday. Your twenty-ninth birthday—that's kind of a big one."

Pete wrinkled his forehead. "It is?"

"The last year of your twenties. Soon you'll be an ancient thirty-year-old. You've gotta live it up, man."

Pete laughed. "All right. Let's do it." Then he did the most astonishing thing—he kissed Jack's cheek, free and easy as anything.

Jack grinned the entire drive back to Pete's place, where they made out again for a minute before Pete reluctantly tore himself out of the car.

"I'll pick you up at eleven," Jack said.

"Okay. Thanks."

Jack wanted to thank Pete for simply existing, but he nodded. "Tomorrow."

"Tomorrow."

Chapter 13

Pete woke up on his birthday with a smile on his face. He'd been having a dream where he and Jack were feeding each other bites of birthday cake. Even if it had only felt like a prelude to what he really wanted to be doing with Jack, it was still a good dream.

He gave himself permission to skip his morning workout and ate breakfast while skimming Lynda Barry's classic *What It Is* for the dozenth time. His sister called to wish him happy birthday while he was deciding what to wear. Jack hadn't specified what they were going to be doing today, but he figured clean black jeans and a gray T-shirt would cover most eventualities.

"Happy birthday, Peter Jacob," she sang into his ear while he put his sneakers on one-handed.

"Thanks, Emily Sophia," he said. "How's life?"

"Same old. How's being twenty-nine?"

"It's actually not that bad." He wanted to tell her about Jack, about the fact that he'd met someone incredible and improbably he'd turned out to be the author of the children's book series he illustrated, but Jack would be there soon, and it seemed way too complicated to get into.

Is this what it would be like for the rest of their lives, having to explain the convoluted story to people when they asked how they first met? With the sort of optimism he hadn't allowed himself in a long time, he kinda hoped so.

They chatted for a minute, then his phone

started buzzing with texts from other birthday well-wishers and Emily had to go. Pete grabbed his wallet and responded to birthday texts while standing in the driveway waiting for Jack.

A text from a number he didn't have on his phone popped up just as Jack's sleek rental pulled into the drive. *Happy birthday, kiddo.* Pete almost dropped the phone.

Kurt was the only one who'd ever called him that.

Jack rolled down the window. "Hey, birthday boy," he said with an endearingly goofy grin. "Hop in."

Pete stuffed his phone in his pocket and stuffed his reaction down, too. He wasn't going to let anything ruin his birthday.

When he got in the passenger seat, he suddenly remembered what they'd been doing the last time he'd been sitting here, barely more than twelve hours before. His gaze dropped to Jack's mouth and then they were kissing, hard and fast. Pete was dizzy—

he wanted all of Jack and he wanted him now.

"Carol's at work," he said between nibbles on Jack's plush bottom lip. "You wanna come in?"

"Of course I want to come in." Jack dropped his forehead to Pete's. He was breathing hard. "But you said slow, and I don't want to rush this, either."

Pete was torn between disappointment and pleasure. As much as he wanted Jack, the fact that he'd really listened to him, really *heard* him, meant that when things got to that point, they'd be ready. "Okay. Sorry. You're right."

"Sweetheart, you don't have to apologize." Jack backed slowly out of the driveway. "We'll get there."

He said it with such certainty that Pete shivered. He'd spent a lot of time imagining what it would be like when they finally let themselves cross that line and he suspected he wasn't creative enough to come close to how good it was going to be.

"So, where are we going?"

Jack was getting on the highway heading east, and for a second Pete worried they were going to the city.

"That depends. Do you like surprises?"

Pete considered this. He used to like surprises, but then he'd gotten too many bad ones in a row. Just a few days ago, the surprise of meeting Jack had been complicated by the surprise of Jack being Jonathan Avery. He bit his lip. "You know what? I think I've had enough surprises lately."

"Fair enough. I thought we could go to Dia Beacon, and then have a late lunch. Or we could eat first and then do the museum if you're starving. It's about an hour drive."

"Dia Beacon?" Pete had never been to the modern art museum in the Hudson Valley.

"Yeah, unless you'd rather do something else. I've only been there once, but I figured it would be up your alley." Jack sounded slightly uncertain, and Pete rushed in to reassure him.

"No, I've never been. I'd love to go. Thanks for thinking of it."

Jack's smile returned. "Awesome."

They spent the drive talking about anything and everything and the hour went by stunningly quickly. The museum wasn't busy on a Monday, and they decided to see the Andy Warhol installation before they stopped for lunch in the cafe. Jack was talkative and enthusiastic about the art, asked intelligent questions, and always seemed interested in what Pete had to say.

They were wandering around the gift shop, Pete's brain buzzing with all the visual inputs, his phone filled with photos he'd taken for inspiration when he next spent some time at his computer or at the studio in the Art Center. He hadn't felt this inspired in a long time. He looked up from a book on Agnes Martin to see Jack watching him.

"What?" He smiled self-consciously.

"Can I take your picture?" Jack asked. "You look really hot with a book in your hands."

Pete looked down at himself, casually dressed, his hair hanging in his face. "Um. Okay."

Jack lifted his phone and snapped a photo. He looked hot, too, in his green button down and the same pair of jeans he'd been wearing all week. They fit snug across his ass and Pete had been appreciating that fact all day.

"Thanks for today," Pete said, setting the book down regretfully. He would have liked to spend more time investigating the pages, but he couldn't justify spending fifty dollars on a coffee table book when there might be legal bills in his future.

"You're welcome," Jack said, scooping the book up. "Allow me." He walked to the register before Pete could protest.

"Hey, you already paid for the museum tickets. And lunch," Pete said, hurrying to catch up as Jack handed over his credit card.

"It's your birthday," Jack said, as if that gave him a free pass to spoil Pete.

He had to admit it felt nice to be spoiled.

He took the book from Jack graciously. "Thanks. Again." He hesitated, then decided to be honest. "This is the best date I've ever had."

"Yeah?" Jack sounded pleased. "Well, it's not over yet."

They drove through the cute little towns of the Hudson Valley, stopped for dinner at a trendy pizza place Jack said Kingston had told him about. They split a bottle of chianti and spent dinner laughing over respective dating misfires of their youth.

Pete felt a little wobbly as they walked back to the car. Maybe the split had been more like 60/40 on the wine. "Are you okay to drive?" he asked as Jack unlocked the car and slid behind the driver's seat.

"Pretty sure I am." Pete caught Jack's playful smile as he closed the passenger door behind him. "But maybe we should make out a little before we get on the road to be on the safe side."

Pete didn't need any further enticement. He

practically launched himself toward Jack and kissed him. He'd been wanting to do that since...since the last time they kissed. Jack tasted like tomato sauce and garlic and Pete wanted to gobble him up.

They kissed hard and deep, the almost filthy wet sounds filling the car's cabin. Jack was a good kisser, naturally, and Pete couldn't physically get close enough. He pulled away reluctantly. "We've got to stop doing this in the car."

"Definitely," Jack agreed. He adjusted his jeans briefly and Pete suddenly became aware of his own arousal. He looked at the dark bulge between Jack's legs and licked his lips.

"How far from Rosedale are we?" Pete asked.

"Almost an hour, I think."

"Fuck. I did not think this through."

"Look—it's probably for the best," Jack said a little bleakly, starting the engine. "We're grownups. We can wait."

Pete buckled his seat belt and banged his

head back against the headrest. He occupied himself on the ride home by watching Jack's hands on the steering wheel, his face lit up intermittently by passing headlights. He was humming along with a song coming soft on the radio, a small smile on his beautiful lips.

"How are you still single?" Pete asked when they were getting closer to Rosedale.

"What do you mean?"

"I mean you're smart and kind and you have a cool job. Oh yeah, and you're hot and not broke. Why aren't you with some super successful corporate billionaire or a Broadway star? You could be married to Anderson Cooper, for fuck's sake."

Jack laughed. "There's no way I would be married to Anderson Cooper."

"Why not?"

"Because I was waiting for you," he said casually, as if he hadn't just said the most romantic thing anyone had ever said to Pete.

"Jack?"

"Yeah?"

"Can you take me back to your place?"

Jack glanced sideways at him. "Why?"

"Because this has been the best birthday I've had in a really long time, and I don't want it to end." It was only partly the truth.

"Okay," Jack agreed. A minute later he turned the car onto Bramble Street, a long rural road with leafy green trees forming a canopy above them that Pete couldn't see in the dark but knew was there. Soon they pulled into Kingston's driveway. He had a cute little two-bedroom cottage set back from the road, a charmingly overgrown garden in the front. They got out of the car in silence. Pete left his Agnes Martin book behind, followed Jack up to the front door. The inside of Kingston's place was essentially the same as it had been the last time Pete had seen it, a few months ago when Kingston was up from the city for the weekend.

"Want a nightcap?" Jack asked. "I got some bourbon at the package store yesterday."

"No, thanks. You go ahead if you want."

Jack went to the kitchen and came back with two glasses of tap water. "You want to sit?" He nodded to the little sitting area.

"I want to take you to bed," Pete said.

Jack stared at him hard.

"I know I said slow, and I know we both have our reasons for waiting, but it's my birthday and I just really want to do something selfish. If you're up for it."

Jack set his glass down on the coffee table. "You're the birthday boy. You call the shots."

"Are you sure? I want you to want this, too."

Suddenly Pete was being kissed. When Jack drew back, his eyes were full of emotion. "You have no idea how very much I want this, Pete. I'd be honored."

Pete swallowed. "Then what are we waiting for?"

Chapter 14

Pete wanted to go to bed with him. Tonight.

A part of Jack thought he should remind Pete why they were waiting, why he'd wait forever if he had to. Another part of him needed to give Pete whatever he wanted. It was Pete's birthday and Jack was more than halfway in love with him—he'd give him a kidney if he asked. Sex wasn't a hard sell.

But his hands still shook as he opened the door to the bedroom. This wasn't some one-night stand or a random guy he'd date for a few months before they both moved on. This was Pete.

Jack couldn't fuck this up.

"You okay?" Pete asked, closing the door behind them.

Jack turned on the bedside lamp, glad he'd taken thirty seconds that morning to straighten the sheets on the bed.

"Yeah." His voice cracked on the word. He cleared his throat sheepishly. "Yes, just don't want to disappoint you on your birthday."

"Why would I be disappointed?" Pete asked. His voice was mild, and Jack remembered to breathe. Maybe he was making too big a deal out of this. It's not like it was their wedding night. Oh god, but there *could* be a wedding night someday. His knees felt weak.

"I don't know." He cast around his brain for something to say that wouldn't reveal too much. He was acutely aware he could accidentally do something to frighten Pete off.

"Isn't birthday sex supposed to be kinky and shit?"

Pete's dimples made an appearance. "It depends. What are you into?"

Jack was certain his cheeks had gone an embarrassing shade of scarlet. He was older than Pete, and presumably more experienced, but he'd always preferred the tried and true in bed to the chagrin of some of his more adventurous partners.

Before he could stumble through an answer, Pete took pity on him. "Let's keep it simple. Birthday or not, I haven't done this in a while. I just want to be with you."

"That sounds good," Jack said, unaccountably relieved. "How long is a while?"

"Since before I came to Rosedale. Maybe like…seven months? Since before I caught Kurt in the coat check with Randy."

Jack hated that the last person Pete had slept with was his awful ex. "Wait. He cheated on you with a guy named Randy?"

"I told you. As cliche as it gets." Pete crossed into Jack's space, cupped his cheek with one of his big hands. "But I don't want anyone else in here with us, okay?"

"Right, okay." See, Jack was screwing this up already. "Sorry."

"Don't apologize." Pete kissed him firmly on the lips. "You want to take off your clothes now?"

Jack barked out a laugh, some of the tension sloughing off. "Is the romance gone already?" he joked.

Pete smiled sharply. "It's just that I've been dying to see underneath these jeans all day." He looped his fingers into Jack's belt loops and tugged him close. "And you make me fucking horny, Jack. Did you know I didn't miss sex for six months until you walked through the door of Hot Brew?"

He'd had no idea. But it was nice to know he wasn't alone in his horniness. And even if Pete wasn't feeling as many all-encompassing feelings as Jack was, at least they were on the same page about this. He could keep this on a physical level if that's what Pete wanted.

"Well, like I said. Birthday boy calls the shots." He wasn't wearing a belt, so he undid the top button of his fly, then took one of Pete's hands and pressed his fingers against the zipper. "Go ahead and open your present."

Pete snort-laughed, but he took Jack at his word and slowly dragged down the zipper. Jack was semi-hard in his boxers, and as the back of Pete's knuckles skimmed the outline of his cock through the material, his dick gave a leap as more blood rushed in.

"I like it when you call me birthday boy," Pete said, opening Jack's fly to frame the bulge in his boxers. He cupped Jack gently. "Maybe that's my kink tonight."

"Yeah?" Jack's voice was rough with arousal. "I can work with that." He realized he was surprisingly unselfconscious with Pete. He didn't want to mess up, but Pete was being easy and playful. He wasn't going to let Jack fuck this up. Not tonight, anyway. He relaxed into the moment, forgetting about the stakes and the pressure of it being their first time. He was about to have sex with an incredible person—an incredibly *hot* person.

He licked his lips. "You want to get sucked off, birthday boy?"

Pete's hand tightened around Jack's almost completely hard cock. "Fuck. Yes."

Jack flipped them around and pushed Pete down on the bed. He unbuttoned his shirt. Pete whipped his off as well to reveal a flat stomach and toned pecs accentuated by a dusting of dark hair. His nipples were hard and imploring Jack to suck them, but he couldn't get sidetracked just yet.

"You want me to use a condom?" he asked, throwing his shirt over the back of a chair. He stepped out of his jeans and socks, having left his shoes by the front door when they came in. Kingston insisted on a shoe-free interior.

"I've been getting tested like once a month

since…just in case, so I'm good to skip it if you are," Pete said, toeing off his own socks. His feet were long and slender like his hands, and Jack really needed to see if his cock made a matching set.

"I'm good—I mean, I'm clean. It's been a while for me, too." Jack couldn't have remembered the name of the last guy he'd slept with if his life depended on it. All he could think about was Pete. Pete was letting him look. Letting him touch.

Letting him taste.

He sank to his knees on the braided rug on the floor and scooted between Pete's thighs.

Pete unbuttoned his fly hastily, shoved his jeans and underwear down in one go. Jack helped him get them all the way off then sat back on his haunches to simply gaze at Pete's neat thatch of dark curls and the cock rising from them. It wasn't as wide as Jack's own, but it was definitely long and pointed straight to Pete's navel, hard as steel. His balls were lightly dusted with hair and that's where Jack started. He nuzzled along the sensitive skin, licking until he hit the base of Pete's beautiful dick. He took his time, painting the hot, hard flesh with his tongue until he made his way to the crown. When he finally slipped the plump head between his lips and sucked, Pete clutched the top sheet on the bed with white knuckles, making hushed moans.

Jack pulled off and Pete's cock sprang back and hit his stomach with a wet slap. He gently grabbed Pete's hands and wove his fingers into his hair. "Come on, birthday boy. Let me hear you."

Pete's next moan was louder, and he tugged experimentally at Jack's hair. The combination of Pete's dick in his mouth and hands guiding his head, the intermittent pain of his hair being pulled, and Pete's increasingly frantic cries had Jack reaching down to grab his own cock by the base to stop himself from prematurely spilling onto Kingston's rug.

"God that feels so amazing, Jack," Pete

said. "Look at you. You're so good. You're perfect."

Jack could tell he was close. He sucked him down as far as he could, and when the spongy head of his cock hit the back of his throat, the muffled gagging sound he made had Pete tightening his grip. "Oh shit. So deep you're choking on it."

That seemed to be a good thing as far as Pete was concerned, and since Jack was enjoying the feeling of Pete using him, he opened wider, took Pete nice and deep, exaggerated the choking noise.

Pete came straight down the back of Jack's throat.

He let out a stream of curses, then suddenly let go of Jack's hair and flopped backward onto the bed, which caused his saliva-sticky, still mostly hard cock to slide out of Jack's mouth. He swallowed what hadn't already slipped down his throat, sighed happily, and got off the floor to collapse onto the bed next to Pete. He hadn't been used that hard in a while.

"Are you okay? Was that too much?" Pete asked, breathless and concerned.

"It was a lot," Jack agreed. "But it was fucking hot."

"Your mouth is—I mean, I'm not a writer, but I could write an ode to your mouth, Jack."

"You're an artist," Jack said. "Remember?"

"I'd love to draw you sometime," Pete said, kind of dreamily. "Would you let me?"

Jack's heart flip flopped in his chest. "Anytime, sweetheart."

Pete turned toward him, blushing pink. "I like it when you call me that, too."

"What?"

"Sweetheart."

Jack hadn't even realized he'd been doing it. But it was encouraging if Pete liked his nicknames. "Good to know."

"Jesus, what about you?" Pete suddenly sat up, looking down to where Jack's hard-on was tenting his boxers.

"Whenever you're ready," Jack said casually. "No rush."

"God, I'm such a selfish prick. But that blow job kind of blew my mind, too."

"It's okay, truly," Jack protested. "It's your birthday, after all."

"Then I want a turn," Pete said, jutting his bottom lip out in a sexy pout.

"Didn't you just have one?" Jack teased.

"No, I mean I want to suck you off."

Jack's dick gave an answering leap. "If you want to."

"I really, really want to. Can I?" Pete's fingers fumbled at the waistband of Jack's boxers.

He nodded and Pete peeled them off. He was naked now, lying on the bed, hard as he'd ever been. Pete straddled his thighs. Where Jack had started at Pete's balls and worked his way up, Pete started at the top. All the way at the top, kissing Jack's forehead, then his nose, then his mouth. He stayed there for a while, then latched onto Jack's earlobe, worrying the flesh in such a way that had Jack feeling it in his desperately hard cock. Jack arched his neck when Pete started kissing his way down the side. Everything was so sensitive, each swipe of Pete's lips felt more intense than the one before.

"You're killing me, birthday boy," Jack said on a growl as Pete licked his clavicle, then his nipples, not stopping for long on his journey down Jack's stomach.

Pete spent some time licking around the circumference of Jack's cock before pulling the whole thing into his mouth in one gulp. Jack's hips lifted off the bed as he bucked into Pete's tight heat. He couldn't help it; his entire body buzzed with electrical shocks, and Pete's lips around his dick was the jolt that was going to finish him off.

"Shit, Pete, oh my god." Jack didn't even know what he was saying as he tried not to come. "Sweetheart, I'm going to—"

Pete pulled off, panting. "Do it, Jack. I want to taste you."

Jack swore and Pete sucked him back down. He couldn't tear his gaze away from Pete's mouth stretched around him, at his hair hanging over his beautiful eyes, at his strong, long thighs bracketing Jack's own. He could see that Pete was hard again—or maybe still—and Jack got dizzy thinking about how many times they could make each other come in one night. It was Pete's hand snaking down to touch himself while Jack's cock was filling his mouth that finally made him shout through his orgasm. "Pete, sweetheart, yes, thank fuck."

Pete pulled off a little. Jack could tell he was letting the come gather inside his mouth. Some of it was smeared along his lips and chin and if Jack could have come again right away, he would have at the sight. He watched Pete deliberately swallow the pool of come he'd collected.

"That was the hottest—" He didn't know how to finish the sentence. He couldn't remember a blow job he'd been that into. This time was different because it was with Pete—

he was so big and beautiful and had so much of Jack's heart already. The sex was just the mind-blowingly hot icing on the cake.

Cake.

"Cake!" he cried, sitting up rapidly.

Pete rolled off and looked at him quizzically. He crooked a confused grin at Jack with his swollen lips. "Cake? Is that some new euphemism?"

"I forgot about your birthday cake," Jack said, struggling to get off the bed. "Oh wait—" He looked at Pete's crotch. His pubes were slicked down, glistening with— "You came again?" he said in wonderment.

Pete looked down at himself, his cock still half-hard against his thigh and shrugged. "Uh, yeah. While I was blowing you."

Jack leaned back in and kissed his dirty, pretty birthday boy. "You're incredible."

"Why? Because I came twice in twenty minutes? I think that just means I was sex deprived." Pete laughed self-deprecatingly.

"No. Because you're you." Jack took a deep

breath, kissed Pete again and decided to take a tiny leap of faith. "I'm kind of really super into you, you know." He pushed to standing, grabbed his boxers and said, "Meet me in the kitchen in a minute?" And he went down the hall before Pete could respond.

Chapter 15

Pete sat staring at the door after Jack left. It was beginning to occur to him how much trouble he was in. He'd been chalking up all of Jack's little endearments and romantic asides to his being a writer—he was clearly a passionate, creative guy. Maybe he called everyone "sweetheart."

But Pete knew he didn't. Jack liked him. A lot. It wasn't a surprise. The shock was in how much he liked Jack back. Jack had relentlessly burrowed beneath his armor, with his perfect mouth and his perfect face and his perfectly un-perfect hair. He'd embedded himself beneath Pete's skin like one of those wicked corkscrew burrs. They didn't hurt so much until you started pulling them out.

Pete swayed. His stomach was in free fall, and not in a good way. From the beginning, Jack had been so careful with him, so clear about his feelings, so free in bestowing his attention, his care, his affection. Even his money. Pete should have seen this coming—that sweet, earnest Jack, for some reason infatuated with Pete, would be able to get beneath his defenses.

Now that he was there, Pete didn't know if he could handle it. Should he just call it off now, before someone got hurt?

He'd told Jack he trusted him, and it was true. He trusted Jack. He didn't trust himself. He didn't trust his judgment and he hated that he was bringing more baggage to this relationship than Jack should have to deal with. Jack was too good; he shouldn't have to deal with Pete's sordid little problems.

He thought of the text he'd gotten that morning. It still made him vaguely sick to think about. He'd changed his number months ago, but it didn't matter. Kurt had gotten his claws in Pete, and he was still bleeding him dry. He was still screwing Pete over if he was paralyzed with anxiety minutes after having sex with someone he cared about.

Sex with Jack was...*pure*. Pure joy. Pure excitement. Pete felt like he could be himself; they'd only touched the very tip of the iceberg with what they'd be up for doing together. All the same, he didn't need anything fancy—he only needed Jack.

And maybe that was the answer. Maybe he could do this. He'd built himself back up from the crushed shell of a man he'd been after Kurt was through with him. After all, Pete was strong, but he wasn't strong enough to turn down the gift of Jack Avery.

And Jack was waiting.

He pushed off the bed and went to the familiar small bathroom in the hallway between this room and Kingston's room at the end of the hall. He washed off the drying fluids with a washcloth, landed it in the laundry basket. He returned to the bedroom, straightened the sheets. The room smelled like sex. He put on his underwear and jeans but left off his shirt. The cottage was warm, and Jack was only wearing boxers.

When he got to the kitchen, Jack was standing by the counter, staring into space, fiddling with a box of matches. He looked up, his eyes a little cloudy. "Everything okay?"

Pete hesitated. "What's all this?" he asked instead of answering.

Jack lit a match, the sulfur smell hitting Pete's nose with an acrid punch, then lit the single candle on the small cake on the counter.

"Happy birthday, Pete," Jack said quietly, pushing the cake across to him.

"No song?" Pete joked weakly. He had no idea how Jack had come up with an actual birthday cake and candle—they'd been together all day and he'd only found out it was his birthday last night —but then, it seemed Jack never met a problem he couldn't solve.

Instead of joking back, Jack started to sing. But this was no typical off-key rendition of "The Birthday Song." Jack's voice was smooth and deep, and it held a country twang that reminded Pete of his childhood. He realized he was holding his breath, not wanting to miss a note coming out of Jack's mouth. He exhaled deeply when Jack finished.

"Of course you can sing, too," Pete said after a beat of silence. "Is there anything you can't do?"

Jack shrugged. "Make a wish."

Pete looked at the flame dancing over the white-iced cake. He was officially twenty-nine. He'd spent the decade making mistakes, learning from them, picking himself up and making more mistakes. But everything he'd done had led him to Rosedale, had led him to Jack. He settled on his wish. Even if he kept making mistakes from now until the end of time, he wished to have Jack by his side when he made them.

He blew out the candle.

Jack got out a knife. "It's kind of late—you don't have to eat any if you don't want to. It's coconut, by the way."

"My favorite," Pete murmured. "How did you know?"

Now Jack looked bashful. "I called Hot Brew this morning and talked to Meadow. She put me in touch with that baker lady—the one who makes the bread? She happened to have one made, and said you seemed to like it at the last Art Center event she was at. Sorry if that's a little stalkery."

"You went to the trouble of getting me a birthday cake, Jack. Thank you." Pete had so many feelings swirling around inside him, getting sugar high on Stacy's coconut cake couldn't make things worse. "When's your birthday?"

"Oh, not until February." Jack cut a wedge and tipped it onto a plate.

Pete helped himself to a fork from the drawer, straddling a stool next to the counter. It was strange to be here with Jack. When he first came to Rosedale, he'd lived here for two weeks, and it had the air of home. But it was Jack's home now, albeit temporarily. What would it be like to truly share a living space with Jack? He'd never actually moved in with Kurt, thank goodness. Though maybe it would have been harder for Kurt to hide all the shitty stuff he was doing if Pete had been in his space more. Pete pushed away thoughts of Kurt and concentrated on the cake. It was moist and sweet and more than taking pleasure in eating it, Pete felt warm because Jack had thought to get it for him.

"You aren't having any?" he asked when he noticed Jack was watching him eat, leaning against the counter and looking like an underwear model, albeit one with messy hair.

Jack wrinkled his nose. "I'm actually not a big coconut fan."

"Oh no." It wasn't fair that Jack couldn't

have any of the cake he'd so thoughtfully arranged. "Well, not that you have to, but it's not a very coconutty coconut cake. It's more of a suggestion than a really overpowering flavor."

He scooped up a small taste, one that avoided the shredded coconut middle layer, and held it up in invitation.

Jack shrugged, leaned in, and took the bite off Pete's fork. Pete couldn't tear his gaze from Jack's mouth as he chewed. God, Jack's mouth was jerk-off fantasy made flesh. He knew how to use it, too. Pete had wanted to come the second his dick was in Jack's mouth, and he'd barely lasted long enough to see how deep Jack could take him. Quite deep, it turned out. He felt himself responding to the sense memory, getting hard sitting on a stool in Kingston's kitchen.

"What do you think?" he asked, in an effort to get his mind off sex.

"You're right. It's pretty good. I'm not a fan of that artificial coconut flavor, but this is mild. More like a vanilla cake than anything else."

"Right?"

Pete put some more cake on the fork and offered it to Jack, who grinned, and took another bite. It was so much like his dream last night, though in his dream they hadn't been in the kitchen, and Jack had been wearing more than a pair of navy cotton boxers. Pete liked reality better than the dream.

It hit him then. He could never have dreamed up someone as perfect for him as Jack. He'd be an absolute fool to let Jack go. And he reminded himself that every time he got nervous about where they were headed, Jack did something to reassure him he wasn't going to turn around and hurt him.

Jack wasn't actually perfect; Pete knew that. But he might have been perfect for Pete.

By the time they finished the slice of cake together, Pete's dick was throbbing in his jeans. Jack licked a stray crumb from the corner of his mouth and Pete couldn't hold back any longer. He got off the stool, boxed Jack in against the counter. He kissed him, tasted sugar and butter and flour. Tasted sweetness. Tasted love.

"You're amazing," Pete said against Jack's mouth. "You're spoiling me."

"Gotta spoil you on your birthday," Jack said between kisses.

Pete stopped kissing him long enough to make eye contact, trying to be as brave as Jack always was. "No, I mean, you're spoiling me for anyone else."

Jack held his gaze. "Good."

This is it, Pete thought as they melted into each other, then sort of collapsed onto the floor, hands grabbing and kneading, mouths tangling, then sucking and kissing marks over chests, arms, bellies.

Pete got his pants off impatiently, and they rutted together, dry but too frenzied to stop for anything to slick the way.

Pete didn't care, he needed the friction, he

needed the heat. He wrapped his hand around both their dicks, tugging and urging Jack on. He'd already come twice tonight, but he felt his third orgasm gather all too soon. Jack stiffened first, his mouth latched onto Pete's shoulder, teeth digging in deliciously hard. The slickness of Jack's come got Pete the rest of the way and while he wanted to take his time, to take Jack apart and put him back together with meticulous slowness, he had to believe they had all the time in the world to get there. He came with Jack's name on his lips.

Chapter 16

After the dream of a day that was his birthday, Tuesday was a return to routine for Pete, for the most part. He had the early shift at Hot Brew, so after waking up side by side at Kingston's, a sleepy Jack drove him home to change. Jack left him in Carol's driveway armed with the Agnes Martin book, most of the rest of the birthday cake, and a firm goodbye kiss.

He felt a little hungover as he put the cake in the fridge and got ready for work. Not from drinking, but from pleasure. His head felt fuzzy, and he wanted nothing more than to call in sick and spend the day in bed with his gorgeous new—

Shit. He'd been about to think the word "boyfriend." He and Jack hadn't talked about anything as far as labels were concerned, but after a handful of dates and one overnight sharing a bed, boyfriend seemed premature.

On the other hand, Pete found himself whistling in the shower, despite his foggy head. What had Jack done to him?

He checked his messages on his walk to Hot Brew. He had a short email in his inbox from an attorney who said they'd been referred by Christopher Avery. Before he could think better of it, he replied that he could talk after three p.m. that day and gave his phone number.

Almost right after he sent the message, his phone buzzed. A text from an unknown number. *Miss you, kiddo. How was your birthday?*

This wasn't happening. Kurt wasn't allowed to come in and act as if nothing had changed, as if he'd done nothing wrong. As if Pete was just going to casually text back, *Hey, yeah, my birthday was great. I spent it with a guy fifty thousand times better than you.*

Tempting, but no.

He stared at the phone for a second, then thumbed to his main message screen and found Jack's thread. *Free for dinner tonight?*

The answer came as he was putting on his Hot Brew apron. *For you? Always.*

He smiled the entire morning so hard his cheeks ached by the time Meadow came on shift at noon.

"You're in a good mood. I take it you got what you wanted for your birthday," Meadow said with a smirk.

"I had some pretty good cake," Pete said, hip-checking her playfully, "thanks to you."

"Happy to help two lovelorn losers get their heads out of their asses and put other parts there instead," Meadow said blithely.

Pete snorted. "Jesus. You know, the obsession you're starting to have with my love life is a little disturbing. What about yours?"

"I actually have a date this weekend with Melissa from the bookshop. So there." Meadow stuck out her tongue, flashing the silver stud in the middle.

"Oh cool. I met her the other night. She seems nice." Pete was happy for his friend, even if it galled him to acknowledge she'd been right all along about Jack and him.

***

Jack: *Working from the cottage today. Hope you don't mind. Meet at Nina's for dinner at 6?*

Pete: *I'll be there. Hope the work goes well.*

Jack: *Thanks, sweetheart.*

Pete was already sitting at a two-top in a cozy corner when Jack arrived at Nina's. He'd lost track of time midafternoon. When he finally looked up from his computer, he realized he'd have to race to get ready, but he refused to show up to a date with Pete in his cargo shorts and faded Walk for the Cure T-shirt.

He leaned down and bussed Pete's cheek before sliding into the seat across from him.

Pete looked fantastic, of course, in a black short-sleeve button down and jeans. He smelled good, too. Jack was pretty sure he wasn't the only one who'd showered before their meet-up. They spent an embarrassing ten seconds smiling goofily at each other before he said, "How was your day?"

Pete's smile dimmed slightly. "Work was good. How about you?"

"Got a bunch done on the book, yeah," he said. "But what else happened today?"

Pete's eyes narrowed. "You know we've only known each other a week," he said out of nowhere.

"A week and two and a half years," Jack reminded him.

"Either way, it's kind of scary that you can read me so well."

Jack reached across the table and brushed a finger over the back of Pete's hand. "Look, I know things have been moving fast, after we both saw the merit in moving slow. But I can't help it. I don't want to pretend like I don't know something else is going on with you. It's probably better if you know now how crazy I am about you."

He'd been thinking about it on and off all day. He didn't want to scare Pete away, but he didn't want to play it cool just because most people would think finding the love of your life in a small-town Connecticut coffee shop was worse odds than winning the Megabucks. Well, Jack had won the freaking lottery and he wasn't letting go of his prize.

Pete took a deep breath. "It's okay. I—I'm glad you can be honest with me. I don't want to be some skittish, needy waif you have to walk on eggshells around."

"That's not how I see you at all," Jack said. "You're strong, and smart enough to know that it's not a weakness to ask for help."

"Thanks, Jack." Pete smiled. Jack would never be sick of that smile. "About that—I talked to the lawyer today."

Jack's pulse sped up. That was huge. He wanted to know everything, but the server chose that moment to take their order.

Pete scanned the menu quickly. "I always get the eggplant parm."

"Make it two," Jack said, smiling impatiently at the server. When she was gone, he asked, "What did the attorney say? Can they help?"

"So it turns out Kurt has a record. He was convicted on some white-collar embezzlement charges about five years ago, in Florida. Apparently, he was skimming off the top of a gallery he worked at in Miami. Basically doing the same thing he did to me. The attorney said it shouldn't be too hard to prove he forged my name to the loan documents, and if I press charges, he could owe me restitution on the credit line I had to pay off. It might be harder to get back the money I loaned him directly, but I've already emotionally written that off."

"That's amazing. You're going to do it, right?"

Pete hesitated. "I don't really want to spend the next several months, maybe years, dealing with this. I feel like he's taken so much from me already."

Jack frowned. He'd respect Pete's decision, but it was hard not to want Kurt to face consequences for his actions.

Pete went on, "But more than anything, I don't want him to be able to do this to anyone else. So if pressing charges against him helps someone else from falling prey to his schemes, then I have to do it."

Jack's chest swelled with pride. God, his boyfriend was so amazing.

Wait.

Pete *was* his boyfriend, wasn't he? Maybe he'd bring that up later, when the conversation was more about them and less about shitty Kurt.

"I'm proud of you," he said. "And let me know what I can do—help with legal fees? Maybe we can get the publisher to give you your advance early or something if money's an issue."

"I think I'll be okay. I appreciate it, though."

Jack knew it cost Pete to say that, and he smiled warmly. "We'll just have to put out another Super Rupert book. Kingston said the publisher is getting ready to offer us a two-book contract extension, if you're up for it."

"I love drawing for Super Rupert, you know that."

"It wouldn't be the same without you, P.J. Blue."

Pete laughed. "Thanks, Jonathan."

When Jack took Pete back to Kingston's later, they didn't discuss relationship labels or lawyers or ideas for the next Super Rupert book. Their mouths were far too occupied elsewhere to talk.

———

From k.james@jamesliteraryagency.com
To jonathanavery@super-rupert.com

The deadline approaches. How's it coming? How is our boy? Do I need to come up there and light a fire under you? Either way, I've been working on that project we discussed a couple of months ago and there's been some movement. I'll be in touch when I have a firm offer.

Kingston

Sergio: *Hey Jack, just wanted to let you know Daisy and I will be in Rosedale this weekend and we'd love to get together if you're still in town.*

Chapter 17

"God, can you believe that rush?" Meadow wiped down the counter, then fanned herself with a menu. They had been slammed all morning with locals and tourists alike who'd been drawn downtown by a flea market being held on the town green.

"I know, and I'm not even supposed to be here today."

Meadow rolled her eyes. "Okay, Dante. Ruth's coming in an hour if you can hang on that long."

Pete worked closing last night and had

been too tired to do anything but fall into his bed at Carol's, since Jack said he was planning to work late on the book. He had been looking forward to a lazy morning—yesterday he and Jack had made plans to make pancakes at Kingston's before checking out the flea market —but Parul called out sick and Pete couldn't say no to his manager's entreaty to cover her shift.

He grabbed a tray of pastries and started restocking the case. "I'll survive. Hey, how was your date?"

Meadow grinned. "I thought you were never going to ask. It was awesome. We went to a show and then to Sparkle in Midville and got a little tipsy."

"The gay bar?" Pete had never been, but it didn't seem like Meadow's kind of thing.

"It's pretty fun. You and your boy should check it out sometime. Speaking of." Meadow nodded at the window overlooking the street. "Isn't that him?"

"Jack?" Pete looked up and got a little jolt

from Jack's unmistakable profile. He was across the street, waving at someone. Pete watched, the flutter of happiness at the unexpected sighting turning into a quiver of confusion when he saw who Jack was waving to. The guy from the woods, Sergio, walked right up to Jack, his smile big. Jack was smiling back. They talked for a second, then started walking in the same direction. Side by side.

Jack hadn't even looked Pete's way.

It wasn't as if Jack wasn't allowed to talk to someone without Pete's permission. And it wasn't as if he'd caught Jack cheating. Jack wouldn't do that. But still, he felt slightly ill as he closed the pastry case and took the empty tray to the back.

He resisted the urge to text Jack. To call him. To run down the street and demand to know what was going on. Because all of that would have been irrational. He trusted Jack.

Pete left his phone in his pocket, took a deep breath, and returned to the front. He'd finish his shift and he'd meet up with Jack and everything would be fine.

The door opened. Pete looked up, half hoping it would be Jack himself. He knew the man coming into Hot Brew. But it wasn't Jack.

It was Kurt.

"Hey kiddo, how's tricks?"

He looked exactly the same as the last time Pete had seen him—the same leather jacket, same rakish salt and pepper beard. Pete was unreasonably angry that the asshole hadn't gotten less attractive in the past seven months.

Kurt smiled, confident and warm. "What? No hello?"

"Hello," Pete said woodenly, over the roar in his ears. It was hard to take a full breath, but he managed to get out a few more words. "What are you doing here?"

"I came to see you. Our mutual friends told me you'd been hiding yourself away in the country. Thought I'd come see if I could tempt you back to the city with me. I have a deal in the works—you might want to get in on it."

Pete closed his eyes. He'd imagined running into Kurt one day, imagined telling him off, maybe even rubbing his face in exactly how happy and well-adjusted he was, even if he had to pretend to be both of those things. Now that he'd met Jack, he wouldn't be pretending anymore. Here was his chance, but all his words had fled. He couldn't think of a single thing to say to the man who'd taken so much from him.

He sensed Meadow staring at him and realized to her this guy was just a customer. He opened his eyes and gritted out, "Unless you're going to order something, you can leave."

Kurt's smile wavered slightly, and he took a step forward. "You don't mean that. I know you've missed me, kiddo."

"Don't call me that. I'm not a kid. And I haven't missed you. I think you should go."

Kurt shifted from foot to foot, his usual

charm seemingly thrown off by Pete's response. "Pete. I—I'm sorry about everything that happened. You know I didn't mean to hurt you."

"You used me, and you knew exactly what you were doing."

Kurt's mask slipped and his smile became a sneer. "You needed me. You practically begged me to take you on as a client. You'd have no career if it wasn't for me."

"I never needed you. I was naive back then, young and stupid. But I know better now, thanks to you, and I have friends who'll back me up." As if to prove his point, Meadow moved closer to his side. "Not to mention legal counsel."

Kurt's sneer hardened. "Yeah. I got a call from your fucking *legal counsel* yesterday. Why'd you gotta play that way?"

So that was what this fake niceness was about. "Maybe we should only communicate through our lawyers from now on, Kurt. I've been done with you for a long time."

Kurt's face went red. "Listen, you little—"

"He said he's done with you. Get out."

Pete hadn't even noticed the door open, but he recognized Jack's voice, even if he'd never heard him use that particular sharp tone.

Kurt turned to look behind him. Jack stood there looking murderously calm, his eyes narrowed to slits as he stared Kurt down. Pete was so tall, he forgot that Jack was tall too, and while he was softer than Pete, he was broader. Right now he looked huge and menacing, even in shorts and sandals. He filled out every inch of his white T-shirt, looking bigger than Kurt, though they might have been the same height, and Pete felt an unexpected rush of lust at seeing Jack defend him so aggressively.

"Who the fuck are you?" Kurt said, trying to sound cocky, though some of the swagger had left his shoulders.

"I'm Pete's boyfriend," Jack said clearly. "And he wants you to leave."

Kurt laughed meanly and twisted his neck

to look at Pete. "Is that what you meant by friends? You're screwing some twink townie?"

Pete almost laughed. He'd never thought of Jack as a twink, and he certainly wasn't a townie. What would Kurt say if he knew Jack was connected to one of the most powerful families in the country?

"I don't have anything else to say to you, Kurt. I'm not going to ask you again. Please leave." Pete held Kurt's gaze for two long beats, drawing strength from Meadow at his side and Jack standing between Kurt and the door. "Now."

Kurt blinked first. He walked slowly up to Jack, who looked fiercer than ever. "I hope for your sake he actually puts out for you. Frigid bitch wasn't worth my time."

Pete heard a gasp, then realized he'd made the sound. His cheeks suddenly felt tight, as the blood rushed to his face in a hot blush.

Jack bared his teeth, balling up his fists at his side. "Get. Out." He spit the words through his teeth and Pete knew he was using every ounce of his self-control not to haul off and hit Kurt across his smug, bearded face.

Kurt waited another beat, as if waiting for the punch. When it didn't come, he stalked to the door, his boots clomping noisily across the wood floor. He flung open the door and didn't look back as he walked away.

Pete watched Kurt go, then rushed around the counter, suddenly needing to touch Jack, to get the reassurance of his skin on his. They hugged hard and then Jack held him away from his body.

"Are you okay?" he asked, running his hands over Pete's back, his arms, as if checking him for physical injuries.

"I'm fine. I'm fine. You were magnificent, Jack." Pete knew he was riding on adrenaline and would crash in a bit, but for now he was just happy to be near someone who cared about him enough to defend him against his horrible ex.

"I can't believe he came here. What a fucking asshole," Jack said, the sharpness back in his voice. "What did he want? How did he even know you were here?"

Pete's relief dimmed slightly. He winced. "He said mutual friends told him where to find me. Whoever he talked to must have given him my number, too. He texted me a few times earlier this week."

"What?" Jack looked shocked. "Why didn't you tell me?"

"I didn't want you to have to deal with even more of my issues," Pete said. "It was—okay, maybe it wasn't the best idea. I didn't think he was going to do anything besides text me. And I took screenshots and sent them to the lawyer, just in case."

"Well, I'm glad of that," Jack said grudgingly. "But seriously, sweetheart, you gotta tell me these things." He reached up and cupped Pete's cheek with his dry, warm palm. "I'm here for you. You know that right?"

Pete's heart rate had slowed under Jack's ministrations. Now it kicked back up. "I know. And apparently you're my boyfriend, too?"

Jack's eyes went liquid. "Um. Yeah. I am. You are. I mean, *we* are. If that's okay?"

Pete's mouth curved up. "It's okay. It's pretty fucking perfect, actually."

Jack's answering smile was enormous and made him look young. Happy. How amazing was it that Pete was the one who put that smile on Jack's face?

"Oh my god, will you please clock out and take your boy home before you get any fluids in the store?" Meadow's voice was dry as dust, but she was smiling.

Pete shot her a look. "Ruth's not here yet. I don't want to leave you alone."

Jack looked at his watch. "And actually, I'm supposed to meet—"

This time Pete did notice the door opening. "Sergio."

Daisy's owner walked into the shop and looked at Pete, and at Jack's hand on his arm.

"Uh, hey guys. Didn't mean to bother you," he said, a little uncertainly. "I was just waiting for Jack and—"

"Sorry, had an emergency," Jack said. "Sergio, you remember my boyfriend Pete, right?"

"Uh, right," Sergio said, giving him a small wave. "Is everything okay? Do you want to reschedule our meeting?"

Pete looked at Jack with lifted eyebrows. What the hell was going on?

"I'll explain later," Jack said to Pete. "Why don't you finish your shift and I'll pick you up after?"

"Okay." He was still confused, but he was fairly sure whatever Sergio and Jack were meeting about was perfectly innocent.

The door to Hot Brew opened again and yet another familiar figure stepped inside.

"Time to pop the Cristal, Super Rupert scribes, because you have the best agent slash friend in the business!"

"Kingston? What are you doing here?" Pete asked just as Jack said, "Hey, man!"

Jack's agent stood there, posture triumphant, in his customary trousers, natty button-down, suspenders, and a paisley tie, his locs pulled away from his angular face by a piece of matching paisley fabric. He was holding a bottle of what appeared to be fancy champagne, though it was barely noon.

"We have celebrating to do," Kingston insisted. He swept his gaze over Sergio appreciatively. "Hello, and who might you be?"

Sergio looked even more confused. "I'm Sergio Ortiz."

"Kingston James," he said. "Are you involved in this little party?"

Before Sergio could answer, Meadow said, "If I get cups, can I get in on the bubbly?"

"Why certainly, Meadow. Bubbly all around."

"What exactly are we celebrating?" Pete asked, deciding the day wasn't going to get less weird from here. He might as well embrace the chaos.

Kingston walked up to the counter, where Meadow was setting out five paper espresso cups. He peeled the shiny gold foil from around the cork. "We're celebrating the offer I just negotiated. A certain studio is buying the film and television rights for the Super Rupert series for a cool seven figures."

He popped the cork with a flourish, but Pete barely heard the noise. He was still processing the number. Seven figures? As in...a *million* dollars?

Kingston poured, Jack whooped, and Meadow clapped happily. Sergio still looked confused, but he took the paper cup with a smile. Pete found a cup in his hand, but he didn't drink. He'd dug up his contract for the Super Rupert books just this week so the lawyer could go over the numbers and make sure Kurt hadn't somehow diverted his earnings away without Pete realizing it. He was familiar with the clause that read he was entitled to 20% of any ancillary rights. So far that had been merchandise in the form of some T-shirts and pencils sold on the publisher's website. This was a whole different level.

"Super Rupert is going to be a movie?"

Meadow asked. "Also, this champagne is wicked good."

"At three hundred a bottle, it better be the best you ever had," Kingston declared, before tasting his own serving. "And maybe. Rights are one thing, getting it made is another. But we get paid no matter what."

"And when you say seven figures, can you be more specific?" Jack asked. "Not to be crass, but…"

"One point eight million," Kingston stage whispered.

Pete swayed. He felt his eyelids drooping as his vision went a little gray.

"Pete, are you okay?" Jack's voice sounded far away. "Oh shit, sweetheart, sit down."

He didn't pass out, but it was a near thing. Pete found himself sitting in one of the hard metal cafe chairs, Jack's hand warm and secure on his back, rubbing circles as he dropped his head between his legs and tried to breathe.

"Jesus, Pete, sorry." Kingston sounded apologetic.

Pete struggled to speak. "No, it's okay. I'm okay. It's just been a day."

Jack chuckled shortly. "No shit. Sergio, Kingston, can you give us a second?"

Jack dropped to his knees, and Pete was able to lift his head and look his boyfriend in the eyes. His beautiful, worried eyes.

"Do you feel dizzy? Want to move to the floor?"

Pete took inventory. His head felt better, though his legs still felt rubbery. "I'm good. I think I'm just a little overwhelmed."

Jack was still rubbing circles on his back. "I'm going to take you home."

"No, I'm okay."

"I want to take you home," Jack said firmly, and this time Pete understood. *Jack* needed this. It was okay for Pete to let Jack take care of him.

"Yeah. Let's go home."

Chapter 18

After Jack trundled Pete into the passenger seat and slid behind the wheel, he turned on the engine and paused, faltering. Where, exactly, were they supposed to go? Jack had said home, but his home had somehow become Pete. And by extension, Rosedale.

But Pete's single bedroom afforded them no privacy, and with Kingston in town, Jack's borrowed cottage no longer seemed like the sanctuary it had been.

He wondered what was currently on the market in Rosedale. How much room would they need? Ideally there would be an office for Jack, and a studio for Pete. Maybe a yard for a dog. And what about kids? Did Pete want them? He would be a great dad. Jack's chest ached with longing thinking about a baby cradled close to Pete's chest, Pete's dimples carving valleys into his cheeks as he looked down at the bundle of life.

Oh no. He was doing it again. Getting too far ahead. So far ahead Pete would probably drop him faster than a hot cup of coffee with no protective sleeve.

"Rosedale has a law against idling for longer than three minutes," Pete said mildly.

Jack looked at him, wanting to give him so much more than he could at that moment. "Sorry. I was just thinking—where's home?"

Pete smiled sadly, as if he knew what Jack meant. "Yeah. Good question." He shrugged. "I don't know, but right now I just want to hide away with you and forget about the rest of the world. Is that okay?"

"Whatever you want," Jack said quickly.

"I want you to take me somewhere we can be alone so I can fuck my boyfriend silly."

Jack's entire body tightened at Pete's words. Agreeing to that was the easiest thing he'd ever done. "Okay."

They stopped at a strip mall so Pete could grab sandwiches from a deli while Jack visited the drugstore to grab electrolyte water, and a few other essentials. They drove out by the highway and checked into a beige, corporate chain hotel where they could disappear into their room and be certain of not being disturbed.

The hotel room smelled like, well, a hotel room, and the interior furnishings were just as bland and beige as the outside. But Jack didn't care about any of that. He could only see Pete. He'd been quiet since they left Hot Brew, but he seemed...calm. At peace. As if he was right where he wanted to be. And Jack couldn't describe how grateful he was that this person had picked him.

There didn't seem to be a rush. They ate their sandwiches and talked about nothing. Jack didn't taste his, but it was still the best lunch he'd ever had. Everything with Pete was like that. It was the best ever, because they were doing it together.

"I'm gonna take a shower," Pete said, standing and stretching so his shirt rode up over his flat belly. He walked to the bathroom door.

Jack's mouth watered, his gaze glued to Pete's ass. "Yeah. You do that."

Pete turned and grinned. "Wanna join me?"

Jack was suddenly shy. Since Pete's birthday they'd been together three times. Everything had been good—better than good. Pete was so unbelievably hot, and he knew what he was doing in bed, no matter what Kurt had implied earlier. It had been a while for both of them, which meant they'd taken their time to explore, to gradually add things to their repertoire. They hadn't showered together yet.

It was an intimacy that Jack was probably ready for.

He was more nervous about the other thing Pete had said in the car. About fucking him. They'd used fingers, but they hadn't gone further. He was a hundred percent sure he wanted to, but they'd only just been able to say they were boyfriends. As much as he needed to give Pete what he wanted, he also had to protect his own heart. He was scared that once they crossed that line, Jack would be in so deep that he might not recover if Pete decided this wasn't working for him anymore.

He'd never had his heart broken before, not really. He'd had crushes on unattainable straight boys, he'd had disappointments and been hurt, intentionally and unintentionally. But all of his experiences to date hadn't prepared him for the enormity of the real thing—being in love with someone who might not love him back.

Jack was in love with Pete. As he sat on the

edge of their hotel bed and looked at him, standing effortlessly beautiful in the doorway to the bathroom, framed by yellow light, Jack had never been so scared in his life.

"It's just a shower, Jack, not a marriage proposal," Pete said lightly. "You don't have to. I'll just get cleaned up and—"

"It's not the shower," Jack broke in.

When he didn't say anything else, Pete frowned. "What is it? I know this day has been kind of extra."

"It's not the day—but yeah. We should probably talk about...everything." He'd purposefully compartmentalized all that had happened since the moment he walked into Hot Brew and seen evil Kurt verbally abusing Pete. Jack had been livid. Yeah. It had been an emotional day. He should probably back off, let things return to normal before he dropped another emotional bomb into the mix.

But he thought he might blow up if he didn't get this out.

"Pete, I have to tell you something first. And the timing sucks. And I already know I'm totally messing up, because I've been so careful, but I...I just have to tell you. And I hope you'll understand."

Pete walked back to Jack, dropped down to his knees so he was almost eye-level. "What is it?" His voice was hoarse. "You're scaring me, Jack."

"I'm in love with you," Jack said, in a rush. "And I wouldn't have cared if that had been a marriage proposal because I fucking already know I want to spend the rest of my life with you. I know we just met, and I know you have shit to deal with and I have my own baggage and we work together, and you don't deserve to have me put this on you so fast, but I had to tell you. Because if you don't think you could ever love me back, I think I need to know now, before—well, it's probably too late for me. But I could save you the trouble. Or something."

Jack stared at the colorless carpet, belatedly realized he was shaking, his stomach abuzz with nerves. He'd never told anyone he was in love with them before. He was pretty sure that was a crappy way to do it, after mediocre deli sandwiches in an anonymous hotel room. He should have waited, made it romantic. That's what Pete deserved. Pete deserved to hear "I love you" for the first time in a haze of champagne and flowers, from a guy who had a speech prepared, not the desperate, pathetic admission of someone who was afraid to lose the best thing he'd ever found.

Slowly, Pete slipped his big hand around Jack's smaller one and squeezed. "Hey, it's okay, Jack." His voice was soft, as if he was gentling a spooked animal.

Jack tried to breathe, wary of letting himself be soothed if Pete was about to break his heart.

"Look at me," Pete said, still soft, but firm.

Jack swung his head up to look at Pete, his expression soft and open.

"We might have just met, but you have

treated me with so much respect and care since the start. There's no doubt in my mind that you do love me. Thank you for telling me." Pete kissed the back of Jack's hand and he relaxed slightly. Pete didn't seem mad, at least.

"I wasn't looking for you, Jack. I was happy on my own, I was making my life work. If you hadn't come along, I would have been okay. But something happened the minute you stepped into Hot Brew. You changed my life. I'm never gonna be the same because of you. Because you showed me what real love looks like. You showed me what my life could be like if I was brave enough to let you in." Pete's smile was dazzling. "It could be so good, Jack. We could be so good together. We *will* be so good together, if you keep giving me the chance to be with you. It might take me a little longer than you sometimes—I'm not as brave as you, I think. But I need you to give me the chance not to screw it up. Can you do that? Can you trust me enough to give me a chance not to break your heart?"

Jack thought he wanted to hear Pete say he loved him back, but this was better. This was Pete acknowledging that they were going to do this together. That their lives were entwined now. The love was there, they had to keep strengthening what they'd only just started to build, and they could have everything they ever wanted.

"I trust you," he said. Pete had always been honest with him about what he could and couldn't do, and even when it was hard for him, he always let Jack in. "And I believe we'll be so good together. We already are."

Pete grinned. "Yeah."

Jack hesitated. "Can I—" He took a beat. "Is it okay if I tell you I love you again sometime? Will it bother you?"

In answer, Pete kissed him, sweetly soft. Jack let his heart fill up from the tenderness of that kiss. When Pete finally took a breath, he said, "Will it bother me if my boyfriend—" He stopped to drop another kiss on Jack's lips. "—and the hottest, sexiest, smartest, kindest man

I know—" Another kiss. Jack's lips were starting to feel over sensitive with pleasure. "—tells me he loves me?" He kissed him again, this time with tongue, and Jack's fear melted away in the heat and promise of that kiss. "You just go ahead and say it anytime you want."

"Okay." He was drunk on Pete's kisses, on the love that emanated from his body, from his words. Even if Pete wasn't ready to say it back yet, Jack knew it was there, growing between them. He knew Pete wasn't going to hurt him. Besides, his love wasn't contingent on Pete loving him back.

"Now, how about that shower?" Pete rose to his feet in one elegant motion, bringing Jack up with him.

The bathroom fluorescents were too bright, so they shut off the light and left the door open, shedding their clothes and letting the little room get steamy with the water on as hot as it could go. It wasn't a huge shower, but they managed to squeeze in, Pete yelping at the temperature of the water, Jack turning it down to a manageable level, kissing Pete's reddened skin better.

It felt easy, as easy as it always did, but Jack's heart felt lighter. He'd told Pete how he felt, and Pete hadn't run. He'd listened and acknowledged that they were going to get there eventually. And while Jack waited, he had Pete in his arms. What more could he ask for?

They kissed for a long time under the spray, water droplets gathering in Pete's hair, dripping off his cheekbones like he was in a sexy European shampoo ad. Their dicks were hard, but they didn't do much about it, just soaped up using the complementary sliver of soap. Jack had some idea where this was going, so he paid special attention to certain areas, making sure he was clean as could be while Pete had his face under the spray. They towel dried, each making fun of the other's hair before they finger combed it to some semblance of normal. Jack hesitated over his clothes, but Pete didn't even glance at him, simply strolled over to the bed and pulled down the covers, exposing soft white sheets.

Earlier, Jack had put the paper bag from the drugstore on the nightstand, and now Pete shook out the contents, a box of condoms and a box containing a bottle of lube. "So much extra packaging." Pete tsked as he got the bottle out and made sure the contents were ready to be expelled. "I should write the company a letter."

Jack got on the bed next to him, kissed him hard. "God, I love you."

Pete's smile was pink and pleased and he kissed Jack back, then pushed him all the way down on the bed, covering him with his endlessly beautiful body.

Jack lost the plot for a while in the pleasure of having Pete on top of him, in the way they fit together, two big guys in a big bed, nowhere else to be, nothing else mattering except the way they made each other feel. They'd been here before, making out with their whole bodies, dicks rubbing together idly, Pete's mouth constantly on the move, apparently greedy to taste every part of Jack he could reach, but this time it felt like they were building toward something besides mutual hand jobs or giving each other head.

He found himself spreading his legs wider, wordlessly inviting Pete in. Pete went so far as to press a hot thumb against Jack's hole, but then he stopped, looked up, his eyes dilated nearly black, his mouth bitten red.

"Actually, I was wondering if you would be open to fucking me first?"

In passing, they'd both casually mentioned that they were up for switching, though Jack had been fantasizing about having Pete's cock inside him long before he knew what it looked like. But if Pete wanted him, he could get on board with that plan.

"Um. Sure. Of course." He sat up, and Pete flipped over on his back. Jack kissed a pretty brown mole on Pete's hip. "We don't have to, at all," he said, just to be clear.

"No, I want to, I want you to." Pete stroked

Jack's cheek gently. "The last time I did this was with Kurt. I really, really want to know what it feels like with you, Jack. I want my last to be you."

Jack's heart stuttered, started up again at a gallop. He had to kiss Pete, or die, so he did, pouring his love into the kiss. He had to show Pete he understood the privilege he was being given.

"Thank you," he said, low and fierce. And then he got to work, using lubed fingers to stretch Pete carefully, thoroughly, until his hole was slippery and open, and Pete was panting like he was mid-marathon. "Okay, sweetheart?"

Pete nodded, spread his legs, and tilted his pelvis up. "Can we do it like this?"

"Of course, whatever you want."

Jack got a pillow, put it under Pete's hips. Pete's dick was red and stiff against his belly. Jack kissed it briefly; it was hot like burning. He licked a stripe up the side. Pete let out a strangled, "Stop."

He raised his head instantly.

"Too good," Pete gasped. "Wanna come with you inside me."

Jack nodded, completely understanding. His own cock felt like it might go off at the slightest touch. Why hadn't they taken the edge off in the shower? It was too late for that now. He had to get inside Pete, had to make this good for him. He had been given a mission, to overwrite the memory of Pete's ex, and he wasn't going to let Pete down.

He put the condom on, grasping himself hard at the base to stanch his need. More lube. And then he was breaching Pete, sliding in slowly, the tight, hot channel squeezing him with glorious pressure he felt right down to his toes.

Pete let out a broken moan when Jack was fully seated.

"Sweetheart, you okay?" he asked, worried.

"So okay," Pete whispered. "Come on, Jack. Please."

"Coming, sweetheart."

He started to move, and Pete moved with

him, canting his hips up so they joined together perfectly, each stroke more satisfying than the last. Pete reached down to pull at his own cock. Jack had the presence of mind to pause and drizzle some lube on Pete's dick, between his fingers. Pete hissed at the coolness on his overheated skin, then groaned in pleasure as he started jerking himself faster, smoother.

"Genius," Pete gritted out.

Jack smiled smugly, even though everything in him was begging to let go and fill Pete up with his release. He held back, keeping up a smooth rhythm, burning the image of Pete's open mouth and arched neck into his memory for all time.

Suddenly, Pete stiffened and Jack ground his cock as deep as he could. Pearly come began to stream out of Pete's cock, smearing all over his hands, catching in the fine hair beneath his navel. Jack was so fascinated watching Pete jerk himself through his orgasm, his own took him completely by surprise. One second, he was screwing tight into Pete, the next he was shouting at the intensity of his release.

With difficulty he slowed, grasped the condom at the base, and pulled out. He left the bed long enough to throw it away, then collapsed next to Pete, who was still breathing hard. His skin was hot all over.

"God you're a furnace," Jack mumbled into Pete's shoulder.

"I know, I'm pretty hot," Pete deadpanned.

Jack didn't bother raising his head, just groaned. Pete chuckled lightly.

"Was that okay?"

"Exactly what I wanted," Pete said. He craned his neck to kiss the top of Jack's head.

Jack could happily have lived the rest of his life in this bed next to furnace-hot Pete, but eventually they'd need food and water and to interact with people from the outside world. He sighed and turned onto his side. Pete looked equally happy to stay put.

"Hey, Jack?" Pete put a hand on Jack's hip, idly stroking circles with his thumb.

"Yeah?"

"Earlier you asked me where home was. Well, something tells me we'll make one of our own. Someday."

Jack would take it. "Someday sounds good to me."

Chapter 19

Pete woke in an unfamiliar bed with the newly familiar weight of Jack pressed into his side. Light rimmed the blackout curtains. He turned his head far enough to see the blue numbers on the in-room alarm clock. Almost nine. He blinked, disoriented. Was he supposed to work today?

He relaxed into the not-uncomfortable bed. It was Sunday and he wasn't on the schedule.

He looked down at Jack's bare arm, glowing softly white in the gray light of the room and smiled. He was a little sleepy, but not tired. Yesterday they'd both seemed content to pretend they were the only two people in the universe, ordering a pizza which Jack paid extra to have brought up to their room, showering again, then Jack had basically begged Pete to fuck him and who was Pete to refuse? The feeling of sliding into Jack, the pretty, pained sounds he made, the way his skin got all red and blotchy and the way he'd groaned Pete's name as he came—fuck. Pete's cock was already half hard from it being morning, but he needed to stop thinking about how good it was or he'd be uncomfortably hard and unable to do anything about it.

They'd fallen asleep around midnight, and Pete had slept surprisingly well. They'd shared a bed a couple of times now, and Jack was a considerate bedmate. He didn't hog the covers or try to smother Pete accidentally in his sleep. He was a peaceful, constant presence. Kind of like Jack when he was awake. Dependable, thoughtful. But no less exciting for it.

Pete let himself think about Jack's speech

from the day before. It had started off rough—Pete's stomach had taken a dive when Jack said he needed to tell him something. He'd been certain Jack was about to say he'd made a mistake, that he didn't want to bother with Pete after the nonsense with Kurt in the coffee shop, that he wanted to be with someone uncomplicated and easy, like Sergio. But he'd gone and said something Pete hadn't expected but wasn't a surprise.

Jack was in love with him.

He knew it, deep in his bones, because he'd been truthful yesterday when he said Jack showed it in the way he treated Pete. He'd been showing him love since day one, and Pete could only be grateful he was able to accept that love for what it was. Kurt told him he loved him, but that wasn't love. He'd been a toy, a tool for Kurt to get what he wanted. Jack only wanted for Pete what Pete wanted for himself, and it made him wonder what he could do for Jack in return.

Jack snuffled and turned his head on the

pillow. Pete carefully shifted to watch him wake up. Jack blinked his long lashes slowly, awareness coming into his body.

"Morning," he whispered into Jack's neck. He smelled of generic hotel soap and sleep-warm skin.

"Morning." Jack turned, and Pete's arms came around him easily. They always seemed to fit together.

"Sleep okay?" Pete asked, pressing a kiss to Jack's jaw. He didn't want to inflict morning breath on him, but he couldn't hold Jack like this and not want to kiss him.

"I slept great," Jack said. "I was up late last night—Friday night, I mean. I turned in the book."

Pete pulled away, stunned. "You turned in the book? That's amazing, why didn't you tell me?"

Jack cocked an eyebrow at him. "Um. We were a little busy yesterday if you didn't notice."

"Right." Pete swallowed. He still felt

responsible for all the drama of the day before. "Well, good for you. I can't wait to read it."

"I emailed you a copy," Jack said. "I hope you like it." This said quietly. As if Pete wasn't going to love every word.

Pete kissed him. "I will. I'm proud of you for turning it in on time."

"I'll ignore the deadline extension and say thanks." Jack's cheeks turned pink. "I just needed a little inspiration from a certain hot barista who also happens to be an excellent creative collaborator."

"Yeah?" Pete had honestly enjoyed their work sessions. He liked getting the peek into how Jack's brain worked, quick and funny, with an emotional underpinning to everything he did.

Pete had always been a bit intimidated by Jonathan Avery when all he knew was the finished product and the somewhat formal emails they exchanged. Now he knew Jack hid behind the august name, too modest to have much ego about his creative work. He wrote because he wanted to reach kids, to entertain them and to make them feel less alone. Pete thought he was wonderful.

"I was thinking we should work together on the concept for the next Super Rupert book," Jack said sitting up, his hair adorably sticking every which way.

"I'd love to," Pete said. "And I suppose we owe Kingston a case of that bubbly for the film deal."

"I knew he'd make it happen," Jack declared. "He told me he'd had some interest, but he was waiting for the right offer. We've got to get you a proper agent. Maybe you need two. One for your illustrations and one for your fine art? Or maybe just a good business manager. I bet Sergio knows someone."

"Sergio?" Pete knew there was no reason to hate the sound of that name on his boyfriend's lips, but still.

"So it turns out Sergio's on the board of this huge philanthropic organization. He's been involved in some big projects, including renovating a historic library in lower Manhattan that was going to get demolished a couple of years ago. They saved it, restored it, and it's a jewel of the neighborhood now. I was meeting with him yesterday to pick his brain and see what options we have for the Rosedale Library."

"You...what?" Pete clearly needed coffee to process what Jack was saying.

"I asked around, and it seems like the insurance company is giving the town the runaround. I talked to my brother Christopher about it, and he said if we could get some political pressure on them to expedite the claim that might help. When Sergio told me what he did, I thought he'd want to get involved, too, since he's got a place here. It just seemed like fate."

"I'm sure Sergio was only too happy to help," Pete said, still not able to let the handsome man's hungry glances at Jack go.

Jack smiled. "You were jealous. I knew it."

Pete was about to deny it but didn't see the point. "Jealous as fuck." He sighed. "Sorry."

"Sweetheart, you don't have to apologize. Just wait until the next handsome guy we meet hits on you. Or girl for that matter. My green eyes aren't just pretty."

Pete stared into Jack's, yes, very pretty green eyes. "You don't ever have to worry about me, Jack. I'm a one-man guy."

"And you're the only one for me," Jack said gravely.

"I didn't really think there was anything to worry about," Pete said, trying to mean it. "I just didn't like how into you he was."

"I think he gets it's not happening. He's seen me with my hands all over you. And he's a good guy, honestly. You don't have to like him, but I hope you don't mind if he and I end up as friends."

Pete hated the idea that he might be as possessive as Kurt had sometimes acted toward him. "Not a problem. I promise."

"Thanks." Jack kicked off the blankets. "God, I need coffee."

Pete groaned. "Me too. We're such addicts."

"Good thing you've got the hook-up."

Pete smiled. Getting Jack coffee was simple, but it was something he could do for him. It was a start. "I know we have to re-enter the world. I'm a little scared to turn on my phone, actually, but thanks for letting us hide away for a while. And thanks again for yesterday. With Kurt."

Jack's expression turned serious. "Please, please tell me if he ever comes near you again. Call me. Call the cops. He's bad news."

"I know. I will. I promise. I just—you were great. I can't believe I was in a relationship with him. It feels like that was a different me, you know?"

"Change is good," Jack said mildly. "And your lawyer is going to make sure he can't hurt you ever again."

"I hope so. You know, when I was with him,

I felt weak all the time, like I couldn't do anything for myself. And now I feel like not only can I do things for myself, I have people to back me up who actually care about me, and that's even better."

"Damn right." Jack's gaze dropped to Pete's crotch. "And right now you have someone who'd like to back you up against a shower wall and give you a blow job."

Pete's erection had gone down while they were talking, but it had no issue getting going again at Jack's words. "Oh yeah? Before coffee?"

"I would happily blow you before I get my coffee."

"Wow, you really do love me," Pete said, joking but not.

"Yeah. I really do," Jack said softly.

They raced each other to the shower.

Chapter 20

Turning on their phones after they checked out of the hotel wearing yesterday's clothes was painful, but it had to be done. Jack checked his texts first. "Looks like Kingston wants us to meet him at his place for brunch. You up for it?"

"As long as there's coffee. I think I'm going into withdrawals."

"Same." His notifications buzzed again. "Huh, my mom's called like three times. I should call her." He put the phone on speaker and turned the car toward Kingston's.

"Where have you been? Did you get your book turned in?" His mom spoke without greeting, her familiar Texas drawl an immediate comfort. He glanced at Pete and rolled his eyes for show. Jack loved his mama.

"I got the book turned in, and I've been with Pete."

"Your illustrator?" He'd filled her in briefly earlier in the week.

"Yes, and he's in the car with me so you can say hello."

"Hi, dear. Jack hasn't told me enough about you, but I'm sure he will."

Pete laughed. "Hi, Mrs. Avery."

"Oh, sweetie, Mrs. Avery is my mother-in-law. Everyone calls me Mama, or Elaine."

Pete didn't appear turned off by the familiarity. He smiled wider. "Okay, Elaine."

"I hope you're calling to finally confirm your cruise ticket. I have to give them the final numbers today."

Pete lifted his eyebrows in silent question.

"Oh right. Um." He took a left turn,

lowered his voice, even though he knew his mama could still hear. "The Austin-based Averys are skipping out on Christmas and going on a cruise. But you and I don't have to—"

"I've never been on a cruise," Pete said. "Where to?"

"The Caribbean," Mama said brightly. "Six days, seven nights. Leaving Galveston December 22nd. You'd be more than welcome to join us, Pete."

Jack cringed. Pete seriously couldn't want to spend Christmas—their first Christmas as a couple —with the entire Avery family trapped on a cruise ship. Jack wasn't even sure he wanted to do that. Besides, Christmas was months away. Even though he had every intention of being with Pete in five months, maybe Pete would think it was too much pressure.

"Sounds fun," Pete said. "What do you think, Jack?"

"Fun? Yeah. Fun. Okay." Anything with Pete

would be fun, even a cruise with his entire family.

"And I can put you two boys down to share?" Mama said shrewdly.

"I'm okay with sharing if Jack is," Pete said, shoulders moving as if he was silently laughing.

Jack rolled his eyes again, this time at his boyfriend. "Of course we're sharing, Mama. Get us the biggest king they have. Pete's a tall drink of water."

"Taller than your daddy?" she asked, surprised.

"Taller than Dad, taller than me."

"Oh my. I surely can't wait to meet you, Pete."

"Same, ma'am. I mean, Elaine."

"Well, we gotta go, Mama." They pulled into Kingston's driveway. Two cars were parked on the gravel drive with enough room for Jack to pull in behind. "Love you."

"Love you, too."

Jack cut off the call before Pete or his

mama could get up to any more mischief. "You really want to do a Christmas cruise with the Avery clan?"

"I really want to do Christmas with you," Pete said. "The cruise is a bonus."

"I knew she'd love you. You're totally going to be the favorite son now," Jack said in mock disgust. "Fine. We'll go and it'll probably be fun but next year I want to do a city Christmas. I love New York at Christmas."

"I used to," Pete said slowly, as they got out of the car and walked up the path to the front door. "But that's when shit started going down with Kurt and it kind of got spoiled for me."

"Hey, do you think you're done with New York forever?" Jack asked the question that had been on his mind for a while.

Pete shoved his hands in his pockets. "I used to think this was only temporary, but I really like Rosedale. I guess I'd be open to a hybrid life, like how Kingston has a place in the city and here, too?"

"Really?"

"Well, yeah. Your whole life is there."

Jack stepped so close to Pete their chests brushed together. "Not my whole life. Not anymore." He kissed him, warm and soft. "Besides, I like Rosedale, too. And I can write from anywhere, if properly motivated."

"Well, then, looks like we have some options." Pete kissed him back, sweet and long.

"Are you guys going to make out on my front step all day or are you going to come in?" Kingston said impatiently after swinging the front door open.

Jack broke the kiss reluctantly, glared at his agent. "As long as there's coffee."

"A gallon of it," Kingston said, then he laughed when Jack nearly pushed him over in his haste to get to the kitchen.

He could smell the coffee, and other enticing food smells, but was surprised by who greeted him from the floor in front of the coffee maker. "Daisy! What are you doing here?" He knelt and gave the dog a scratch on the chin. He got a slobbery lick on his palm for his trouble.

"She's with me," Sergio said, walking in carrying one of Kingston's oversized mugs.

"Hey, good to see you. Sorry about bailing on our meeting yesterday," Jack said, straightening up and giving him a wave. He felt a little self-conscious knowing that Pete was right—Sergio *had* seemed interested in him, and he'd sort of played into that both to test the waters with Pete and to get Sergio to meet with him about the library. He wasn't a saint. "It was an emergency."

Sergio waved a hand carelessly. "It's all good. Kingston explained. Is Pete okay?"

"I'm great, thanks, man," Pete said affably, appearing in the kitchen with Kingston close behind. "Which reminds me, Kingston, how's your mom?"

"She's doing much better, thanks. Driving my sister crazy, which is a good sign. Food's on the back porch."

"You cooked?" Jack said in disbelief. Kingston was a foodie, but he usually left the cooking to the professionals.

"Sergio here is a great cook. He gave me a hand," Kingston said casually, scooping up a stack of napkins from the counter.

"It was more the other way around, but Kingston makes a pretty good sous chef." The wink Sergio threw Kingston was unmistakably flirty.

"Does he now?" Jack grinned. It seemed he didn't have to worry too much about Sergio's feelings. Kingston could be extremely charming when he wanted to be, and it seemed his charm had worked on Sergio just fine. "Can't wait. We're starving."

"I just bet you worked up an appetite," Kingston threw back at him, glancing at Pete. "Let's eat."

They helped themselves to coffee then wandered to the porch, where a feast had been laid out on a round wooden table. They filled their plates from the towering stack of hotcakes, the bowl of fruit salad, and the crispy plate of local sausage Sergio had picked up at the farmer's market on his way to Kingston's that morning.

Apparently after Pete and Jack ditched them at Hot Brew, Kingston had talked Sergio into a late lunch that turned into drinks that turned into dinner. Sergio had to get back to Daisy, so he didn't spend the night, but Jack read between the lines and could tell his agent and his new friend were getting along like a house on fire.

As they ate, Jack explained to Kingston and Sergio what was going on with the library and how he hoped they could help.

"But...you've barely been here two weeks. What's with the savior complex, Jack?" Kingston's eyebrows merged in confusion.

Jack shrugged. "I like libraries. I like Rosedale. This town deserves a great library. If we work together, rebuilding could start before the end of the year."

"Oh my god, you're going to move here,

aren't you?" Kingston said. "Last year I lost my friend Reed when he moved back to California. Then Pete left, now you. New York is losing all the cool people."

"Hey, I'm there on weekdays," Sergio reminded him. "If you ever need company."

"And I might be a weekender, too, at least for a while," Jack said. "Until I can sell my apartment and find something here. It might take a while to find the right place in Rosedale."

"Why's that?" Kingston asked. "Bachelor like you should be able to find something pretty easily."

Jack looked at Pete. If the man was signing up for Christmas with Jack's family, talking about real estate shouldn't be enough to scare him off. "Well, we'll need a studio, an office, a guest room or two. A kitchen with room for one of those outrageously expensive commercial espresso machines."

Pete's smile spread bigger the more things Jack listed off.

"A yard for the dog," Jack added.

"The dog?" Pete sounded more excited than scared.

"Wait, you two are moving in together?" Sergio said. "I know it's none of my business, but Kingston said you only met like two weeks ago?"

"Two weeks and two and a half years," Pete corrected, draping his long arm around Jack's shoulders.

"It feels longer," Jack said, looking up at his boyfriend's handsome face. He felt a little sorry for his past self, having to go through life Pete-less.

"It does," Pete agreed, gazing at him fondly. "And now we have all the time in the world."

Jack's world hadn't been the same since he walked into Hot Brew. He laughed, thinking about what had brought him there.

"What's so funny?" Pete asked, dimples showing.

"Just that I'm really glad I had writer's block."

Pete's dimples deepened. "Cheers to writer's block," he said, raising his coffee mug.

"Cheers to new friends," Kingston added, raising his mug as well and grinning at Sergio, who raised his in return.

Jack tapped his mug against Pete's. "Cheers to us."

And they all drank.

Epilogue

One year later

"Well look who we have here," Meadow said, lifting her already perfectly arched eyebrows. "Paul, right? Or is it Patrick?"

"Fuck off, it hasn't been that long," Pete said a little defensively.

Meadow relented and smiled. He walked around the end of the counter to give her a big squeeze.

"Just miss not having to get the ladder to get cups from the top shelf," she said with a put-upon air. "Since you quit, the step ladder has been getting a lot of use."

"I miss you, too," Pete said.

He did miss the daily routine of Hot Brew, but he had put in his notice after he and Jack got back from the surprisingly fun Christmas cruise with the Avery family. That's when pre-production started on the Super Rupert animated series, and he'd had to fulfill his role as the artistic advisor. They based the animation style on his drawings, and while he didn't actually do any of the animation himself, he'd helped them get the look of the characters right, mostly remotely, though he'd flown to Los Angeles a couple of times for meetings. He'd never been to the West Coast, and he'd found L.A. a cool city to explore.

It had been that kind of year, whirlwind and full of new experiences. The fall had been adjusting to a new normal with Jack eventually going back to the city to put his place on the market, staying at Kingston's when he could make it back to Rosedale. Pete finished the illustrations for the fourth Super Rupert book in record time, and they made their deadline so it could make its winter release date. It was the best-selling middle grade book of the holiday shopping season, and they'd signed their contract for books five and six.

Which is why his boyfriend had sent him on a coffee run.

"Hey, can I get an Americano and an extra double shot to go?"

"Jack's on deadline?" Meadow guessed.

Pete smiled. "Book five is due Monday, but the library dedication is this weekend, so he wants to turn it in today."

"Oh yes, how could I forget. The Blekitny-Avery Reading Room dedication. You guys are like town celebrities now, aren't you?"

"Does that mean we get free coffee?" Pete asked hopefully.

Meadow rolled her eyes and tamped down the grinds for the espresso shots. "You know I can't take your money."

"Aw, I knew you cared." Pete returned to

the customer side of the counter and quietly slipped a twenty into the tip jar while Meadow was grabbing a lid for the Americano. "But you and Melissa are coming to the dedication, right?"

"Mel wouldn't miss it," Meadow said. "But what I'm waiting for is my invitation to the big housewarming party you and Jack keep saying is going to happen. I've never even seen your place."

"I know, we've been so busy, and the work on the studio just finished. It's almost ready for prime time, I promise. Labor Day?"

"That's in forever! Your birthday is next week, why don't you do something then?"

Pete bit his lip. Jack had mentioned the same idea a couple of weeks ago—a combination birthday/housewarming where they could invite all their Rosedale friends and folks from the city, too. Pete had hedged. It wasn't that he didn't want to show off the beautiful home he and Jack had created. But he'd been looking forward to having it to themselves for a little while after dealing with contractors and workers coming in and out practically every day since they closed on the place that spring. The last piece of work had been finished earlier that week, and they hadn't had a minute to celebrate, since Jack had been frantically finishing the manuscript.

They hadn't even had time to figure out how to use the fancy espresso machine they'd bought for their gleaming, remodeled kitchen. They had a drip coffee maker that worked fine, but Hot Brew still had the best coffee around.

"Soon, I promise," Pete said, leaning over to kiss Meadow's cheek. He grabbed the two cups. "Thanks for these."

"Don't be a stranger," Meadow called as he left.

Their new place was too far to walk downtown, so Pete got into his car, another new addition to his life. He'd bought the hybrid SUV for himself after the judgment came down against Kurt.

God, he was so relieved all of that was over.

His lawyer had worked with the city attorneys and uncovered an entire web of art-related scams Kurt was implicated in. He'd been indicted on several charges and was still awaiting trial, but in the matter of the credit fraud he'd committed involving Pete, he'd already pled guilty and been ordered to pay restitution. Pete's credit had been completely fixed. Even better, some of the charges came from Kurt's time in Los Angeles, so he'd be remanded there after New York had their chance at prosecuting. With luck, Pete would never set eyes on Kurt again, and with Jack and the entire Avery clan at his back, he was finally starting to believe that phase of his life was well and truly over.

He drove past Bramble Street, mentally waving at Kingston, who had promised to come for the library dedication. Thanks to Jack's advocacy, with help from Sergio, Kingston, and several of the Art Center patrons, they'd finally made progress late last year on the library rebuilding project. There was still a lot to do, but the main building had reopened a month ago, and the middle-grade reading room that he and Jack had donated the money for was officially opening this weekend. They'd been so lucky; Super Rupert sales were mind-bogglingly high since news of the TV show broke and would probably go even higher once it started airing. They wanted to give something back, and it wasn't hard to decide on the library as the first place to start.

Pete turned onto Wild Rose Lane, caught sight of the flowers that gave the street its name climbing profusely over the post and beam fence that surrounded their place. This time last year, Pete would have said buying a house with his boyfriend would have been a pie in the sky fantasy, but when it came to signing on the dotted line, he hadn't hesitated. Jack was it for him, he'd known it far longer than he'd been willing to admit, and every step of their relationship had been scary in the best possible way—scary because it felt so right, because it made him so very happy to take each new step.

Their year had been so busy, they'd barely had time to talk about what they were going to do now that things were calming down. The library project was mostly out of their hands, the Super Rupert show was someone else's baby, and the house was basically finished.

He hoped they'd be able to spend some downtime together. They hadn't had a chance to properly look for a dog to add to their family —it would be a rescue, of course. And Pete had been thinking about kids. Maybe not for a while, but they'd both taken one look at the upstairs back bedroom and quietly agreed it would make a perfect nursery. They weren't ready now, but Pete knew they'd get there. And when that time came, he'd be only too happy to grow their family even more.

Jack was his family now. They'd traveled to Texas when Emily graduated from college that spring and done the whole Blekitny tour of San Antonio. Jack had charmed everyone, and they'd eaten too much, and it had been nice to see his parents. But he'd been more than happy to return to Rosedale, construction chaos and all. They had their own little universe here, and Pete didn't take it for granted one bit.

He let himself into the two-story cape-style house, checked Jack's ground-floor office, but, not surprisingly, he wasn't there. He'd taken to working on the upstairs balcony off their bedroom in these warm summer months. The balcony overlooked their backyard, a canopy of green trees surrounding them on all sides, shielding them from the neighbors down the road. Their own private sanctuary.

Jack was there, hunched over his laptop, hair mussed, in a T-shirt with holes along the neck seam, ratty shorts, and barefoot. He was the best thing Pete had ever seen.

"Brought reinforcements," Pete said quietly, so as not to disturb Jack if he was mid-sentence. He sat the cups down on the table, started to back away, but Jack grabbed his elbow, pulled him down to give him a kiss. Pete kissed back out of habit, and almost allowed himself to get lured all the way down to Jack's lap, but he laughed and moved away just in time. "Hey! You have work. I won't be responsible for you missing your deadline."

"I'm almost done, I promise," Jack said, sticking his bottom lip out in an exaggerated pout. "But fine. Can I kiss you after I turn it in?"

"You can do whatever you want to me after you turn it in," Pete said.

Jack's eyes darkened and he licked his lips. He looked like he wanted to reach for Pete right then, but instead he reached for the bigger of the two cups. "You always know how to motivate me."

"That's because I love you."

Jack always smiled when Pete said that as if it was a delightful surprise, even though Pete had told him he loved him approximately five thousand times since he'd screwed up the courage to tell him the first time.

It was on his first trip to New York since he'd left the city wounded and broke. They'd gone so Jack could sign the closing papers on his apartment. Pete had been nervous to go back, but it hadn't been that bad. He avoided his old neighborhood and he and Jack walked around holding hands in Central Park while the leaves changed colors around them. They met up with some of Jack's friends, who were cool, and spent one afternoon at the Metropolitan Museum of Art, where Pete took Jack on a tour of all his favorite pieces. They were in their hotel room getting ready to go out to dinner when Jack walked out of the bathroom half dressed, his hair a mess, talking about some painting he'd really loved from their trip to the museum and Pete had just known.

"I love you," he said, when Jack stopped talking long enough for him to get in a few words of his own.

Jack turned pink, smiled the same smile that he'd just given Pete here on their balcony, like he'd been pretty sure but not totally sure until Pete said it out loud. "Oh," he'd said. "I'm glad." And then Pete had kissed him, and one thing led to another. They'd been so late for their dinner reservation they lost their table and had to eat mediocre food truck tacos, but even so, it was one of the best nights of Pete's life.

"So how close are you?" he asked with studied casualness.

Jack slurped from the Americano and made a satisfied sigh. "With the caffeine— maybe an hour?"

"All right. I'm going to take a shower and I'll wait for you in bed. Naked."

Jack groaned. "Fuck. Okay." He made a shooing motion with his hand. "I'll be there soon."

"Good. Now drink your coffee and get back to work." Pete leaned down and gave Jack one more kiss for luck. And for love.

I hope you enjoyed *His Coffee Shop Crush*! For more feel-good, small-town m/m romance, subscribe to my newsletter at **ellewatersauthor.com** and get a free story! For the next story set in Rosedale, check out *Cool for the Summer* featuring Jack's cousin Beck.

Happy reading!

xoxo, Elle

About the Author

Fueled by chocolate and canned wine, Elle Waters writes steamy, feel-good, small town romances with guaranteed happy endings. She lives with her family in Connecticut. Sign up for her newsletter at ellewatersauthor.com to hear about her next release!

Elle loves to hear from readers at elle@ellewatersauthor.com.

facebook.com/ElleWatersAuthor

instagram.com/ellewatersbooks

amazon.com/~/e/B091FZQ4PZ

bookbub.com/authors/elle-waters